Praise for

EVERYBODY HAS A STORY...

THESE ARE OURS....

" Audrey Lewis does a phenomenal job with this collection and leaves her readers wanting more".

-Red City Review

"Stories. Everyday as we go through our lives we encounter many people. As this collection is titled, every person has a story. Some stories are written onto pages. Audrey Lewis introduces us to these people and then writes their stories onto our hearts."

- Tim Purk, Artist, New York

"Audrey Lewis writes brilliant stories. Some, dark, intense, and a vivid look into the depravity of the human mind. Others inspiring hope and touching the heart deeply. Stories, like none I have ever read, that are both riveting and chilling. For those of us who study the behavior of the human animal, these stories remind us of those who may cross our paths in real life. Audrey hits the nail on the head as she describes what can go wrong and right in humanity."

- Dr. Karyl Lounsbery, Counselor and Assistant Professor
of Counselingat Northern State University

"Expect the unexpected from the talented Audrey Lewis. Filled with highs, lows, thrills and mysteries, her essays remind us of why we read and write and of the power of stories to inspire and entertain. This collection will delight anyone who has ever loved a book."

- Cindy Schaefer, columnist, the Raleigh News & Observer

"Audrey Lewis writes stories touching your heart with emotional feelings that will have you laughing one minute and crying the next. One of the best new author voices I have read in years."

-Dianne Helm, CEO Helm Publishing

"Audrey's compassion and heart shows in her work. Her stories are spellbinding and touching... and will surprise you."

-Karl Ackermann, Entertainment Executive New York

"Audrey Lewis has written a wonderfully imaginative, often quirky and sometimes dark collection of short stories. Everyone will recognize something of themselves in her characters' emotions, struggles and disappointments and they will delight in the stories' often surprise endings"

-Mary Reed, Writer & Marketing Consultant, Austin

"I felt like Audrey was sitting on my couch telling me about real people. While connecting emotionally with the characters, a growing uneasiness began to settle in my mind and heart. In some of the stories, the conclusion left me stunned. It will be awhile before I can let them go."

-Connie Regan, Cook Memorial Public Library, Libertyville

"Audrey Lewis in an excellent writer whose short stories are carefully crafted to keep the reader emotionally involved with her characters as they move rapidly to face a dramatic climax."

-Giovanna Breu, Freelance writer/journalist, Chicago

EVERYBODY HAS A STORY... THESE ARE OURS...

Short Stories

AUDREY N LEWIS

Pressing On Press, Inc.
Libertyville, IL

Pressing On Press, Inc.

P.O. Box 6212

Libertyville, IL 60048

Thank you for your support of the author's rights.

ISBN - 978-0-9862213-4-7

Library of Congress Control Number: 2014956774

To those who inspired, who believed, who gave me strength and who I love unconditionally.

A special thank you to Cindy for the extra encouragement and push to make it real.

CONTENTS

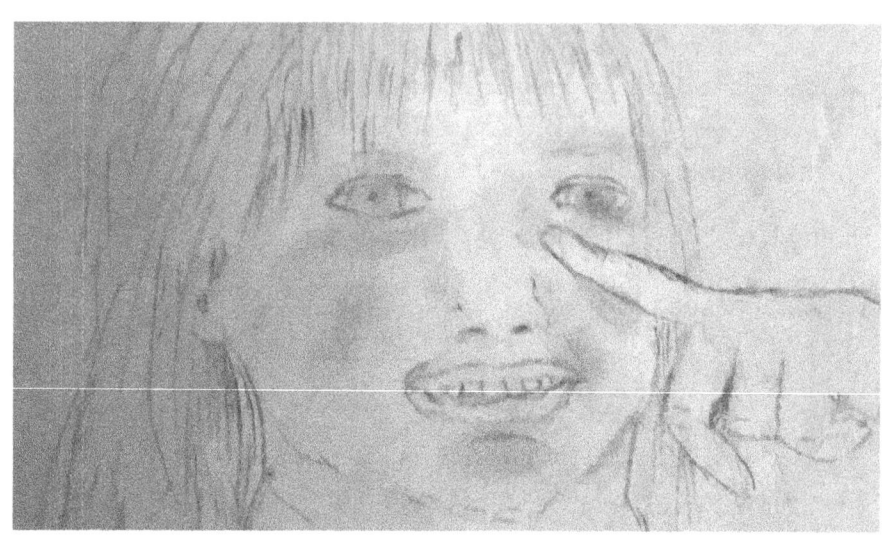

SIMPLE THINGS

Something as simple as this child's strained cry is often all I need to remember how the challenges of daily tasks can burden my soul, should I allow them, and Something as simple as this child's smile is often all I need to be reminded of the smallest of joys, the flutter of the butterflies wings, the warmth of the suns' rays, the rainfall, shallow panting of a dog on a hot summer day.

Simple things that this child does remind me of all that I am blessed with, day to day, minute to minute, this thing we call Life!

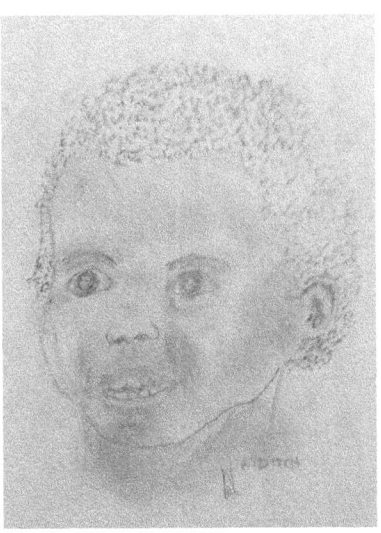

If I put one foot behind the other and keep walking

will I reach yesterday?

THE CLOSET

The Closet

Growing up, my favorite stories were ones about big families. I remember thinking about them often, wishing that one day I would have a big family of my own. I loved playing pretend and had umpteen imaginary children for whom I cared. I protected them from the children who bullied me and I never let them get hurt.

As I got older, I realized it wasn't so much how big the family was, I just wanted to be a mom. How I got there didn't matter, but to have children of my own, now that was important. When I met Michael, there was no question that he was the one and when I said "I do," it was motherhood I agreed to just as much as being his wife. So I was thrilled when nine months after the wedding, Marcus was born.

Marcus, my first born; he was the epitome of the perfect baby. He almost never cried, not even when he was hungry. We could take him anywhere, anytime; he was fine with being on our schedule, even if we didn't have one. He smiled at almost anyone or anything. He didn't mind if other people held him; he always seemed happy. He began sleeping through the night when he was just three weeks old. I remember getting up just to check on him, he was that good. He was the baby that God gave me first so that I'd want a second.

I had always loved kids and wanted a houseful. It was an easy decision when we began trying for number two. However, unlike with Marcus, it was a bit of a challenge getting pregnant. After trying for a year, my doctor suggested testing. Both Michael and I were not quite up to par and I began a series of cycles using the fertility drug,

Clomid. It made me irritable and after several months, Michael was tired of performing in a jar. Just when we decided to discuss how much longer we could continue the protocol, we got word it had worked. I was pregnant.

Marcus had just turned four and loved to watch Mommy's belly grow. He'd pick me flowers and make sure there were extra ones for the baby. He'd try to share his favorite foods and toys; he would lie on my belly and have conversations, with whom he was quite certain was his "baby sister."

I couldn't have been happier when our daughter Alexia Katherine was born. I could hardly wait to take her home and dress her in all those cute little girl outfits. Have tea parties with her, play house, protect her, teach her the virtues of womanhood, become her friend.

She arrived three weeks early, weighing in at five pounds, one ounce and nineteen inches. She came out screaming. When they placed her on my chest and I tried to comfort her, she screamed louder, squirming as best she could to get away, while I tried to hold her tight. In the hospital, she screamed. On the drive home, she screamed. When Marcus met her for the first time, excitedly and proudly waiting with Grandma at the door, holding a pink stuffed kitten he had picked out all by himself, she screamed so fiercely that she caused him to drop the kitty, putting his hands over his ears. I think that was the first time I saw Marcus really cry.

For more than nine months Alexia Katherine cried nonstop, except for the thirty minutes or so when she would cry herself to sleep only to wake up and start all over again. I had read about babies with colic and I had heard babies scream in restaurants. I always thought there was something the parents could do and silently told myself I could do better, that would never be me. But here I was helpless, exhausted, and feeling like a failure.

The upside was that despite her screaming, she always looked precious. I loved putting her in Gap dungarees with a pink and white onesie. Yellow dresses with blue tights, black-and-white dresses that screamed, one classy baby.

I attempted to take her grocery shopping, to breakfast at our local restaurant, to watch Marcus at his T-ball practice and games. I usually got aggravating looks from people and every once in a while, a sympathetic stranger offering bits of advice.

"Try turning her upside down and around counter clockwise. Maybe she's just off."

"Sometimes a pacifier dipped in brandy is just enough."

Enough what? I wondered, but was afraid to ask.

"Precious baby, too bad she's so unhappy. Is she sick?"

I'd taken multiple trips to the pediatrician. I'd asked my mom's advice. I'd even asked Michael's mom. No one had any suggestions and no one offered any relief. The one time I was so sick that I couldn't even muster the strength to get out of bed, Michael had brought her to me, arms outstretched with a squirming and screeching Alexia Katherine an arm's length away.

"Really, you need to take her. I'll take Marcus out for dinner. We'll be back soon." He didn't even wait for a response, didn't offer me anything to eat, or a choice; he just laid her in the bed on top of me and left. That was the first time I really realized I was in this alone. No matter what, it would be up to me to comfort or control, laugh or cry, but always love this little bundle of parental joy, who even then seemed so full of anger. The first day Alexia Katherine awoke in silence, Marcus asked if we had given Alexia Katherine away. I took his hand and together we went into her room to peek.

Marcus excited, asked, "Mommy, can you hear the birds singing?" and indeed I could.

Marcus was so forgiving, and seemed oblivious of the previous months' anguish. He helped me all day, changing her diapers and feeding her; he played blocks with her and read her stories. He was so happy to finally have an opportunity to fill the big brother role. And just like that, Alexia Katherine began to fulfill my dream of the perfect daughter, the perfect baby. Soon, she giggled as often as she had screamed. She quickly went from crawling to pulling herself up and on her birthday, we not only celebrated her turning one, but she took her very first steps independently. Within a day or two, she was running. Life was good.

Marcus entered kindergarten early and Alexia Katherine, Lexi as we soon began calling her, spent hours looking at books and coloring anything she could manage to draw with and on. Once that included the contents of her dirty diaper, obviously a wakeup call to begin full-time potty training.

She was precocious, and her artwork reflected that. She never drew stick people, but full bodies with all the parts, vaginas and penises included (I was never quite sure the significance of that with a two-year-old) and each person always had a different expression. She didn't talk until she was able to speak in full sentences. She loved to collect. She collected things: pieces of grass, buttons, but her favorite and most important collection were the little pieces of paper from the spine of a spiral notebook. We would find these scraps in tiny purses neatly lined up on the floor in her room. Ironically, she seemed to know just how many were there and if we were to remove any, it would send her into a rage, Marcus found this skill hysterical and would often torment her by taking one or two out just to see if she'd really notice. Of course, she would and go off into an uncontrollable rage.

I took her to mommy-and-me classes, but she always just stayed by my side or wandered off by herself. Even then, I noticed she had a difficult time interacting, which brought up painful memories of bullying I had received when I was little. I never wanted either of my children to experience that pain.

4

Preschool was a combination of laughter and sorrow, when once again Lexi couldn't make social connections, but instead would come home and mimic teachers and classmates to a tee. She was strong; she could wrestle with Marcus and would often win, contrary to his insistence that he let her. But she was definitely not athletic and her lack of athleticism would often present itself as uncoordinated and clumsy, making her the last one to be picked for team sports. When she did get picked, it was always followed by comments like "Eww, Lexi smells," or "Do we have to have her?" or "Lexi, Lexi, do or die, we'll put bugs in your eyes." I wonder if that was where she drew her fascination with bugs.

It was especially difficult as she entered the third grade; her episodes of rage came more often and without cause. She would sit quietly in class until it was time to answer a question or participate in a discussion. It did not sit well with her when she was told she was wrong or out of turn. The teachers felt her outbursts were disruptive. Her classmates tormented her on the playground and she didn't know how to respond, so she would retreat into a ball until an adult would come to her rescue.

Teachers and administrators argued with us that she didn't show signs of a learning disability regardless of the fact that she could read at a ninth-grade level but couldn't add two plus two. When we asked that she be tested, they were firm in their beliefs. We had her tested independently. She was all over the place. Her IQ went from forty-five to one hundred eighty. There were no answers or explanations and no one could support the findings with such inconsistencies. We took her to doctor after doctor, specialist after specialist to get help, as it became increasingly difficult for Lexi and for us to deal with her increasing episodes of rage. More than anything, we wanted to find the cause. I begged to know what I was doing wrong so I could fix it. But the answers came in spattered medical jargon, which boiled down to unknown diagnosis. One psychologist told us that we should find skills to protect ourselves as the portion of Lexi's brain that filtered such behavior was undeveloped and drugs or therapy would be a waste of time and money. The neurologist explained that she felt safe in the home environment and therefore was able to let loose of any control she had during the day. Was this supposed to make me feel good? My daughter felt loved so it was okay for her to destroy us, to lash out and destroy everything around us.

I hated how she began to withdraw. How she hated going to school, how embarrassed Marcus was at her very presence in his life at school. Michael buried himself at work and we saw less and less of him. So, like a good mother, I made the necessary arrangements to homeschool Lexi for a while.

In the beginning, it was fun. Lexi loved keeping a journal and reading books that interested her. We did math that incorporated real-life calculating, and real-life adding and subtracting, multiplying and dividing. She became fluent in Spanish, teaching herself and tormenting me when she got angry; she would only speak Spanish, knowing I had no clue what she was actually saying. She loved science, mostly anything that had to do with chemistry. She loved to help in the kitchen so she could see what she could add to what to set off some type of chemical reaction. But what she really liked was hiding some fruit or small crumbs that would attract fruit flies and bugs so that she could crush them. She never minded doing the dishes, as water comforted her, and she would wash them over and over until someone like Michael would complain about waste. This drove her to an obsession with cleaning. The cleaning compounds became much more exciting to mix than cooking ingredients, and some days the smell was toxic.

It was during the time I homeschooled Lexi that she decided she wanted a hamster. She talked about it constantly. It wasn't just that she wanted one, but that she had to have one. I sat her down and explained the difficulties, responsibilities, and commitment of raising a live creature. I also reiterated that as a non-lover of rodents, I knew nothing about their care, nor was I interested in learning. The deal was that if she could show real responsibility with things like her behavior and personal hygiene, and was able to research the ins and outs of hamster care, we would consider it. I left it at that.

After a year of homeschooling, we had both had enough. Lexi developed episodes of rage, followed by fits of crying and needing to be held and loved, with what seemed zero recollection of the rage. I found a new school where she could start fresh and Marcus would be undisturbed by her awkwardness. At the school meeting, she shined. She was little Miss Personality, sweet, attentive, and engaging; the staff and teachers were excited to have her. The students, however, seemed to notice something odd about her from the start and kept their distance. I worried, but knew she needed to get back to normalcy and socializing. She excelled in her classes—even math became easier—but she would rant in Spanish when someone didn't agree with her. When the teacher would ask her to stop, she'd just get up and leave the classroom. No one seemed to know what to do or how to cope.

At the end of that first year back in school, Lexi had come home excited and begged me to sit down. She wanted to show me something. She had put together an entire twenty-minute PowerPoint on the advantages of having a hamster, which included a timetable and monthly cost of its care. She was so very proud in a smirk sort of way, but I couldn't say no and we began that very afternoon to prepare for its arrival. We bought all of the necessary equipment: the cage, the bedding, and an exercise wheel and water feeder. Lexi had surprisingly already cleaned up a space in her room specifically for its housing and care. She had a plastic box filled with newspapers she had been collecting, and carefully laid some in the tray underneath the cage. I remember her stepping back and admiring its perfectly clean environment.

"She better keep it clean," she had said, "or else." How had I missed that? We went back the next day and she picked out a brown and white female, which Lexi named "Blinky." I must admit it was sweeter than I imagined and Lexi seemed to have maternal instincts I had never seen before. I was a bit concerned getting a female, having watched how quickly they multiply, but the sales person assured us that there had only been females in the cage.

Once again, life was good, at least for several weeks. Even Marcus shared in some of Blinky's adventures as Lexi liked to call each excursion out of the cage and into the clear hamster ball that Blinky went in and rolled around the room. When Michael was home, he even pitched in with stories of his own and the gerbil he had growing up. Lexi found it hysterical when I said, "I didn't know that there were gerbils that long ago." But it was on a day that the house was particularly quiet and I was going to ask Lexi to go for a walk that I walked in her room to find her pleasantly engrossed in watching Blinky eat the babies she had just given birth to. Really, how does a mother respond to a scene like that? The truth is I didn't respond, I didn't say anything. I left the room and went in my bathroom to vomit. The look on Lexi's face was not one I would care to describe or even remember. I never mentioned it to her or anyone else; there was a discomfort and disconnect that was best left alone.

But two weeks before school was to start again, I was home alone, enjoying the peacefulness, straightening up, and cleaning. Marcus was camping with his friend's family and Lexi was with Michael's parents for the day. She loved visiting them and especially loved Michael's dad, Stan. Years earlier, when Marcus and Lexi were little, he had an old milk truck, one of the big shiny silver cylinder ones. He had put it out in the field, cutting out windows and doors, adding wood and steel here and there, and making an amazing playhouse for Marcus and Lexi. They named it the Milk House. Sometimes I wished it was mine and I could hide there amongst the field of dried-up corn from when it had once been a working farm. Stan had separated the trailer from the cab just so there was no chance of the kids starting up something by accident; he kept the cab in the barn and would tinker on it every now and then.

I went into Lexi's room to gather her laundry and clean, when I couldn't help but glance over at Blinky's cage. It seemed unusually quiet, and there she was laying very still, her head cocked in an unusual position almost separated from her body. I got closer, knowing what I already suspected. Blinky was dead. I didn't know quite how to react. Should I get her out and dispose of her? Should I call Michael or the doctor and tell them my suspicions? Should I call Lexi or confront her when she got home? I was too scared to do anything so I left it alone, waiting to see what Lexi would do. She did nothing and when Blinky started to smell, I called a psychiatrist, praying they would have answers that the other doctors had failed to give. And after an unemotional Lexi and I buried Blinky, we had our first appointment.

I was told to stop walking on eggshells. Lexi had impeccable manipulative skills and convinced doctor after doctor that she was a sweet little girl who had just been curious. I was the crazy neurotic mom who couldn't discipline her own child. Was it me who was nuts, or maybe they were as afraid as I was? How could they tell me not to walk on eggshells? They hadn't seen her face or lived in the house with her. They didn't offer a diagnosis, drugs, or help—besides weekly meetings that made no advances. Not walking on eggshells only proved to escalate Lexi's behavior.

It was the night she looked me in the eyes, her stare cold as ice. She told me how she was "going to cut us all up in little pieces and watch us all bleed to death... and I'm going to love every second." There could be no words to express my emotions, the chill that ran down my spine. I was afraid of the unknown, afraid because no one seemed to understand. Seconds later, she fell into my arms, sobbing, "I love you, Mommy. Mommy, hold me. Mommy, I love you." With a broken heart and feeling sick to my stomach, I held her, as afraid to let her go as I was to keep her close. Michael was no help and I didn't want Marcus to know, I made an emergency call to each of the doctors who had treated her. Terrified, I relayed the story. Each of them in their own way told me I needn't worry,

"It was just a phase."

"She was having a slight absence seizure and didn't know what she was saying."

"She was trying to see what it would take to push your buttons." It was that very scenario that made me realize I really was alone.

That night and every night thereafter for almost an entire month, I would close her bedroom door and sit just outside of it on the floor, some body part touching it, in case I nodded off to sleep. There I waited in fearful anticipation.

Life went on. Marcus continued sports and after-school activities; he stayed away more than he was home, embarrassed that Lexi might act up or say something too odd to explain. Stan let Lexi fix up the Milk House where she began raising aquariums full of "Drosophila melanogaster;" the same fruit flies she had loved to crush years earlier were now her prized possession. She was breeding them, changing their colors, attempting new hybrids. She kept everything immaculate and one was only allowed in by invitation, even Stan. But with this new hobby also came several years of normalcy. Or at least life without fear. Lexi and I would spend days out shopping, having tea and crumpets, getting mother-daughter manicures. She would confide in me about boys she liked and gossip about who was "doing who" always followed by "Isn't that gross, Mom?" It felt good to have my daughter around, especially after Marcus went away to school. Lexi and I became even closer. She watched out for me, she reminded me of appointments and business meetings. She reminded me when I hadn't seen my friends in a while to call and make plans; she encouraged me to take classes with or without her. But you know, I don't remember her ever really asking me to go with her to the Milk House where she still spent much of her spare time, especially after she got her driver's license and could go there by herself. The relationship, I suppose, was a bit lopsided, with Lexi usually getting her way. It was walking on eggshells that I had found most helpful in avoiding confrontation with her and therefore avoiding flare-ups and rages.

It was years later, when two boys walked into Columbine High School and killed thirteen people, wounding twenty plus more, that the years of painful memories resurfaced. All I could think of was those poor, poor parents, how hard to have to live with what their precious boys had done. Oh, I loved Lexi, just like I imagined that they loved their boys, with the love of a parent for a child that is an unexplainable emotion that cannot be broken.

Lexi went off to college, bringing an aquarium full of her fruit flies with her. Her roommate wasn't too thrilled when they met, reminding me once again of Lexi's inability to conform and her awkwardness among her peers. They lasted the first month, until Lexi began reverting to her old habits and the body odor was unbearable. Her roommate moved out and Lexi found herself once again alone. She waited weeks before reaching out and letting me know. I offered to come down and keep her company but she wouldn't have it. I could hear her holding back tears, something she hadn't done for a very long time. Five days later at four o'clock in the morning, she came home. She didn't say anything, just unpacked her bags, set up the aquarium, and crawled into bed next to me. When she woke up she held me, smiled and asked, "What's for breakfast? I'm starving." The next few months were wonderful. Lexi helped around the house, laughed, smiled. She tried to interact with Michael and began communicating with Marcus. She signed up for classes at the local university and got a job in the chemistry department doing odd jobs. She was happy; she seemed to be on a mission and life was good. Chemistry became a love for Lexi, with biology a close second. She loved having the extra time in the lab and was able to use the lab materials after work. Like most things that Lexi liked, I could see her beginning to not just love chemistry, but began obsessing. Instead of coming home, she would go from classes or work to spend time in the Milk House. Stan had helped her clean it out and she excitedly donated most of the aquariums still full of her precious "Drosophila melanogasters" to the biology lab; the chemistry lab had no use for them. When she also got rid of the aquarium at home, I had mixed feelings. While it was great to have them out of the house, I had been as proud of her as she had been of herself when she had perfected altering their color. Now I wonder if I was closing my eyes to the signs, or did I acknowledge the signs but was too afraid to ask questions. Should I have said something, asked her if she was sure, maybe not seemed quite as excited?

We began to spend more time together; she joined me on walks, where she became obsessed with the large swarms of what we called "no see-ums." They would be in swarms that while I could almost not see them, I could feel them all over my skin. I knew she was plotting; she was missing her aquariums and their content. She wanted to examine my arms when the next day they were covered in bites. She was sympathetic, in an odd sort of way. It wasn't long after that, that she bought several new aquariums, filling not only her room with them but the Milk House as well. On our walks, she carried large sterile jugs that she used to collect swarms of "no-see-ums," who I later learned actually have a scientific name, Ceratopogonidae. She was excited when she shared her findings, and declared that on an average day, a runner or walker passing by would probably ingest two to three hundred of them a day, if not more. "Actually," she stated, "it would depend on the breaths and the depth of the breath, how many one would ingest, and of course how many swarms one passed through."

On rare occasions, she would ask me to help clean up the Milk House a bit; she and Stan were attempting to convert it back to its original state so that they would once again be able to use it as a moving vehicle. Stan had kept the engine up to date all these years and was excited to finally take it out of the barn. He was tickled when after he hooked it up to the trailer, Lexi had asked him to give her driving lessons and she had become quite proficient in driving it. Lexi had come up with a plan. She wanted to take it to the 4H shows and use it as a traveling teaching lab of sorts. She had Stan sold on the idea, but as I helped clean and paint, happy that she wanted to include me, deep down I was a bit skeptical.

As the Milk House renovation got closer and closer to being complete, Lexi's aquariums of Ceratopogonidae grew. She began working on various experiments with them, keeping detailed journals, which no one was allowed to see. It became a bit disconcerting when I noticed her new obsession with the effects of mustard gas and the chemicals used in warfare. She talked about it with enthusiasm, discussing techniques to develop antidotes. As she was close to graduation, she decided to apply to grad school, choosing to take as many classes as possible on-line. She applied for internships to pharmaceutical companies that developed drugs used in executions.

She "borrowed" protective gear from the chemistry lab so that she could work on projects in the Milk House and made it clear that NO ONE was allowed in without her knowledge. She had bought several old box fans and salvaged several metal containers, which she moved into the Milk House, and had spray foam by the gallons, which she used to seal off any door or windows while she was inside. She was ecstatic when she found and bought an old working gas mask on eBay. She told us that she was quite certain the military would be impressed with her discovery.

She began asking Michael questions that she knew he couldn't answer, once again making him uncomfortable and pushing him away. It was just before Marcus was to come home for his five-year high school reunion. Lexi knew if Michael wasn't comfortable, he'd stay at work or need to travel and she'd have more time with Marcus to herself. Lexi spent as much time with him as he would allow. They reminisced, pulled out the Monopoly board, and played for days. They laughed together like they hadn't in years. She asked him to help a bit with the painting of the Milk House; it still wasn't complete and Lexi thought Marcus might have some design ideas. It seemed so normal and once again for a very short time, life seemed so good.

But when Marcus left to go back to home and work, for the first time in years, Lexi totally withdrew. She didn't shower daily, didn't change her underwear, and didn't do the dishes. She didn't go to work or the Milk House, and she wouldn't let me in. Again, like other times, she snapped out of it as quickly as she fell into it, and I found myself walking on eggshells, afraid.

Then, like magic, life changed. I don't remember ever having seen Lexi so excited. Like a balloon ready to burst, Lexi displayed a new persona. Her high school was recruiting volunteers for an upcoming sunrise 5K for the graduating class two years her senior, some of the same kids who led the torment against her in grammar school. She had forgiven them, chalking it up to childhood ignorance. She jumped at the opportunity, throwing herself into it, making what one may have mistaken as sincerity as she attempted working with others on the planning committee. For the first time that I can remember, there were phone calls for Lexi and get-togethers. She would giggle. She called Marcus to chat about new experiences and the possibilities of having others help her finally finish what they couldn't with the Milk House painting. She pushed herself to get the Milk House ready for its first exhibition, which she planned to introduce the morning of the run. She even recruited the committee members to put final paint touches on the exterior, never once letting anyone inside. Stan watched from a distance, proud of his granddaughter and happy to see her enthusiasm being shared by someone other than himself or me.

Those few days prior to the 5K were a whirlwind. Stan checked one last time to make certain that the trailer was secure and the tires full. Lexi had secured the "exhibit," still not letting anyone inside or allowing anyone around to watch her in her preparation. She was anxiously excited. She made all of us "promise not to come." She "needed to do this all by herself." She'd call us when the run was over and we could all go for breakfast. Stan loved the idea; he wasn't loving mornings as much as he used to and it was a bit of a drive so he would have had to rise early. I was worried someone would hurt her and it would backfire. I worried that my little Lexi would once again be hurt, but believing in her, I, too, agreed. She was gone before dawn—I know because I was up not long after sunrise and was surprised when I glanced up from the kitchen sink as I prepared my coffee and saw someone running down the street. As the figure got closer and I realized it was Lexi, my heart sank and my stomach lurched. She ran through the door before I noticed what she was wearing.

"Mom," she cried. "Hurry, follow me!" Frantic, she took my hand, pulling me into the back room and into the empty utility closet. She had planned this, how did I miss it? How did I not see when she had emptied it? She pulled me in and closed the door behind us; she stuffed a blanket at the bottom so no light would come through. Together, we leaned against the back wall, grateful for some room between us. I needed to breathe, to know what she had done. I was sure walking on eggshells no longer mattered. She leaned in toward me and I pulled away. "Lexi, what have you done!" I had tried to say it calmly but it came out yelling.

She stood up, leaning over, got in my face, and with a blank expression, she screamed, "I put bugs in their eyes!! All of them!!" And then, like years earlier, without warning, she fell into my arms, sobbing, "I love you, Mommy. Mommy, hold me. Mommy, I love you." With a broken heart and feeling sick to my stomach, I held her, as afraid to let her go as I was to keep her close. And this was where we stayed for what I'm quite sure was several hours. I could hear the distant sirens and I was sure I could hear the screams. The phone rang several times, and I wondered if it was Michael. Had the news already reached him or did Marcus know? Perhaps it was Stan wondering when we were going to meet him, believing that this couldn't be real.

And then there was the banging on the door, police demanding their way in. Lexi had fallen asleep looking like a troubled angel and I gently moved her, hoping beyond hope that she wouldn't wake up. And as I exited the closet the house filled with an army of gas mask-faced SWAT, their guns drawn. I held up my hands and gave up my baby. As they cuffed her and led her away, she looked back at me with the vacant look I knew so well and smiled that Lexi smile, "I love you, Mommy."

I hope she heard me muster the strength to tell her, "Lexi, I love you too."

The next morning the front pages were covered with photos of Lexi being led away, not even trying to hide. The headlines read: "Genius uses bugs to deliver nerve gas at 5K benefit, hundreds dead."

silent and sleepless
my body aches
the coldness, the emptiness
and the loneliness
the room
where I sleep
seems so very large
and the leftover smells
my only comfort
I ache from the emptiness
of the person I sleep with
I ache from his absence
I try to close my eyes and let sleep envelope me
yet it is hopeless
this feeling is too strong to sleep
my body aches, the coldness, the emptiness, the loneliness
this room where I sleep is suddenly too large

my body began to shrink, shrivel up as the dragons
shadow came over me
first came disappearing smiles
then blackened eyes and piercing my ears was all my stored
pain
somewhere I thought I could reach out
and stand straight, foolish I was now nothing
it was all a dream.

groping into space for an answer
a hope....a moment to be
sparked by a touch
NOTHING
I remain where I am
nowhere

Oh
beast of
mankind
came out of
his shell
without warning
care was
beyond
with fist
raised
up to
worship the sky
he
(beast of
        wickedness)
happily
        danced
                away.

CHAMELE'S RULES

Sometimes there are words or phrases that seem to define us. Such is the case when the following was burnt into my soul.

"Close your eyes and hold on tight
Ya don't want to get stuck behind the light
'Cause if you do, the blackness will swallow up all
them good memories of you
They'll get themselves lost and bring you nothing
but pain, making you wonder if you're even sane
That blackness will hold you
A prisoner for life
If you don't find a way back through the light."

Those were the words whispered to me by Chamele as she sheltered me from the blackness of day in May, 1965. I remember holding her hand so tightly that when I finally opened my eyes, I thought I had turned her white. It was that day that I learned these were words I must always hold dear for how else would I ever remain free.

I had forgotten so many details, or just filed them in a safe place, but now with the anticipation of the upcoming total lunar eclipse, they poured out. I knew that this might be my final chance to save Claire, to reach out and pull her through the darkness, to help her find her way into the light.

I was an age so young that there was only innocence. There was only love, only trust. I was an age so young that I called her Mommy; I didn't even know Mom or Mother. Her words were truth. She was my core and I worshipped her.

Mommy had just gotten home and Chamele met her at the door; it should have been a head's up that I was in trouble but my stomach was still singing from the Cajun Magic cookie I had taken off the rack as they cooled. They were the cookies that no one could ever watch Chamele prepare. It was that magic ingredient that made my stomach sing for more and my heart want to dance; they made me smile as I ate them and laughter filled my voice when I was done. So when Mommy wanted to talk to me, I already knew I was in trouble. Chamele had always told me, "It is a sin to take that which was not mine unless I asked," and now surely I would burn amongst the devils. I had sinned. I had taken without asking. So the day Mommy told me I should always obey Chamele, the family maid and my caregiver, that was the scariest day of my life. Perhaps, as it turns out, it was also the most important. Even that day had its happy place.

Chamele was Cajun and grew up in Mississippi. When she loved me, the warmth of her huge soft breasts were a pillow, comforting, protecting. But when she was angry, they became ominous. Huge black caverns that enveloped me, burying me deep, suffocating. There was no middle, no halfway. There was nothing halfway about Chamele or what she believed. And so following Mommy's orders, I learned to believe everything too. I suppose that it made sense then, that when I started school, I cried dry tears. Chamele had always told me, "Real girls wouldn't show their weakness by letting others see them cry. Real girls must be strong, and stoic. Only real girls grew up to be women, get married to rich successful men, and have children of their own."

Every day, the teacher would take attendance, calling out each name. When she got to Abigail Stern, everyone laughed, taunting, pointing, chanting "dummy." I'd look around, trying to imagine that these cruel chants weren't aimed at me. I'd reach for my happy thoughts, sitting in Mommy's lap on Wednesday afternoons. Her hands soft and smooth, free of household cleaners or dish water. She'd read me "The Lonely Doll" by Dare Wright. That was always how Mommy began. Title and author, she wanted me to remember. She'd brush my hair back off my face, her fingers just barely touching my cheek. It was that soft touch that I cherished most, how like the butterfly's flitting wings, it would almost but not quite tickle. She'd pull me back against her chest; it wasn't soft like Chamele's and I could feel her heart beating against my back. I liked that, the rhythm so reassuring. She'd smooth out my dress and make sure everything was just so, and then brought her face close to mine, almost cheek to cheek. It was my happy place.

Happy places were places Chamele always told me to find, the places where I could always go, no matter what. Chamele told me in no uncertain terms that I was never allowed to lose them. Just like I was not allowed to be bad, or step on cracks, or share secrets or get lost behind the light. It wasn't until much later that I would discover how many happy places I could have and how hard they might be to get to. It wasn't until much later that I would understand the meaning of Chamele's rules.

Back to the chants. How could I respond? My name was Girlie. How could I possibly be Abigail? Chamele called me Girlie and I don't remember hearing any other name in my reference. Mommy didn't refer to me as anything, although when she read to me, she'd always whisper, "I love my little girl," before beginning the story. "Once upon a time…" Sometimes I heard her mention the baby; I think she might have been talking about me. I knew I'd have to respond, to pretend I understood. Although it was with trepidation I'd have to ask Chamele, I needed her permission to be just Abigail.

And so it was, although to this day I'm not sure who truly initiated it, or if that even mattered; the truth is, it was and it did. My coming out party, so to speak. Chamele planned the menu of all my favorite foods, her holiday Cajun chicken, fried sweet potatoes, and itty-bitty biscuits soaked in butter and molasses. Mommy got balloons and had them filled with helium. She and Chamele strung crepe paper around the dining room. I wore my light blue dress, the one with the touch of pink petticoat. I had brand new ankle socks with lace edging and Chamele had helped me polish my black patent leather shoes. We even used the fancy dishes with the hand-painted flowers—the ones Mommy only used on very special occasions, because they were from England. There were fresh flowers everywhere and the house smelled glorious with the various scents all mixed together. And of course on the sideboard was the tea set that had been Mommy's when she was a little girl. I looked at it enviously, knowing it was "look don't touch," but like Chamele said "Girlie, no one ever got in trouble for dreamin'."

Yes, this was my party and when my sisters Claire and Mika came home, I greeted them excitedly at the door. Just their presence filled the house with bliss. The quiet of Chamele and me, overpowered by their very being, Mommy's elation at them being there, even Daddy would hang around for a bit of conversation when they were home. And so it was, so blissful, until Chamele did it; she took my hand and pulled me into the kitchen. She told me to wait until she called me proper; she wasn't happy that I had ruined the entrance. Tears welled up in my eyes, my hand stinging from her grip. I wondered why no one saved me, not even Mommy or Daddy stopped her. I could hear the giggling through the closed swinging door. And then I heard Daddy's voice deep and melodious "da da da da." It was magical. Then Chamele's voice, "I'd like ya' all to meet Missy Abigail Stern."

I waited, hoping to hear Daddy again, but instead, it was Chamele's voice a little louder this time, "Introducing Missy Abigail Stern." The laughter grew louder. I could hear Chamele's heavy foot-steps approaching over the laughter, the swinging door opened and she stood over me, towering. She knelt down until we were eye to eye, she put her hands around my arms, careful not to make any marks, and she shook me, "Girlie, didn't you hear my calling you? Iz a introducing you AB-I-GAIL." I cried dry tears as I put on my painted smile and skipped in to make my entrance, curtseying ever so slightly as I had been told and rehearsed over and over again with Chamele. Claire and Mika erupted in full laughter, Mommy and Daddy, unable to restrain themselves, joined in. Even Chamele laughed so hard I think she farted. The house sung with laughter, laughter that slapped me in the face and stung my soul. Laughter aimed at me, Missy Abigail Stern. But Chamele taught me well, so well in fact that I've even allowed parts of that day to become some of my happy places.

Sometimes I wonder if it was Mommy's ordering me to listen to Chamele that worried me or if I listened for fear of losing Chamele. Like Edith, the lonely doll, who was afraid if she was bad, she'd lose Mr. Bear and Little Bear. I worried that if I wavered, like Edith, I'd be left alone. So I learned how to play by the rules, which included not being bad. I'm not even sure I knew the difference. I followed Chamele's rules, which meant keeping secrets. It wasn't hard to keep Chamele's secrets because no one understood like Chamele. I remember we were playing Sorry and I had just picked my fifth Sorry card in a row, we both started laughing. It was the laughter I loved most, the one where you could feel the tickle in your heart. The laughter that caused Chamele to double over in that deep soul-felt laugh. On this particular day, just like that, she stopped. She got all serious with that peaceful serenity like the angels were talking. She reached over and touched my hand, gently. I think she thought maybe I'd heard them too. But instead, she just said, "Can you hear that... can you hear yourself growing... God is watering your soul."

Sunday mornings were Mommy and Daddy's time, no time for children. Although there were some Sundays when I came home and found Mika or Claire or both sitting in the living room or around the dining table with them talking, eating treats, and laughing. Sometimes they watched television or played a game. Maybe it was most Sundays, perhaps every Sunday, but for certain, Sunday mornings at home seldom, if ever, included me. So I was Chamele's responsibility, which gave way to secrets. My Sunday mornings were Chamele's secret Sundays. I spent Sunday morning with Chamele at her church. I was the whipped cream in a sea of chocolate pudding. It was my energy and enthusiasm, which lacked complete rhythm that brought the loudest singing, the biggest hugs, and what I know today to be the grandest of community laughter. I was Chamele's gift to her congregation. It took years for me to realize it was my lack of coordination and rhythm that was what welcomed me, never my enthusiasm, and never my energy alone. And so while at the time, I believed this to be my happy place, a place where friends overflowed, I would discover that my true friends might only be the Father, the Son, and the Holy Spirit. It wasn't until years later that I understood that my actions inside and outside of church were often calculated by the words of wise old Mabel.

Mabel, who next to Chamele looking like a caramel-colored Jolly Green Giant, held me on what little there was of her lap. She wrapped her arms around me, rocking me back and forth, sheltering me from ridicule as I cried dry tears from the laughter of the congregation. She would tell me "it is not our actions that will be judged alone, but how much laughter we can share with the world around us. Sweet, sweet, Abigail, you share so much laughter, you've already sprouted your angel wings."

Was it the church itself or what it taught? Was it Chamele's wanting me with her or the gift of laughter I created? Laughter which stripped me of any self-esteem. Was it secrets alone that kept me or having secrets to keep? Whatever the answers, it didn't matter for with every negative incident, I worked that much harder to be good, to follow the rules, Chamele's rules, and to find my happy place.

I remember when Claire came to the house on Tuesdays for her "Daddy date," my heart would sing, and my breath would flutter. She would come early, hours before Daddy would arrive and spend time with me. When I was little, it was playing board games and Barbie dolls, and as I got older, so did our activities. Claire showed me how to apply makeup, taught me what was fashionable, she shared intimacies about her boyfriends, and introduced me to my first cigarette. Claire was more than my sister. She was my idol. But secretly, she was also my rival; she was the one who made Daddy smile. The one Daddy spent his extra Daddy time with. Claire was the one most like Mommy. She could be a perfectionist, sing praises through clenched teeth. She was the one Mommy invited into the kitchen to cook with. She was the one Mommy planned shopping days around, always what was convenient for Claire's schedule. Even Mika couldn't compete. I always remember Mika being so astute and focused. Mika was driven, giving little time for Mommy and Daddy, or me. The one thing I was certain Claire didn't have that I did, was Chamele. In the early days, when Claire came to the house, Chamele would stick around close by, listening, and watching, to some degree, I guess protecting. Later, I remember Tuesdays became the day Chamele spent a few hours alone. I remember with rather consistent frequency when Claire arrived, Chamele would go off by herself, Chamele would say, "Always true, a happy you. Twists and turns and someone burns." I'd smile and Claire would glare.

When Claire began bringing boyfriends home, I would wonder which boy went with which story I had been told. Sometimes I would giggle. Daddy wasn't a big fan of Claire's friends. The less he liked them the more she'd bring them back. Chamele always said, "Those you hold dear may not always be near, so see with your heart."

I wonder when Claire forgot how she made Daddy smile. How she warmed his heart and brought sunshine to a rainy day. How she glowed knowingly at his adoration. Claire always told Chamele to fix something extra special on nights she brought boys home for dinner. I remember how much I could tell Chamele was troubled, not because she had to make something special, but because Claire never asked. "Be kind, treat folk the way you'd want 'em to treat you." As harsh as Chamele could be, I think I must've known her heart was always in the right place. Chamele took pride in me, I'm pretty certain of that. Chamele wanted me to turn into a fine woman. And so it was and that made me contemplate what could have happened to make Claire forget, to erase all her happy places. Was it a Sunday outing with Chamele, when I missed some event that altered our world? The sadness in Daddy's face was undeniably a memory that had no happy place. It was a time that stopped the rotation of Earth long enough to send Chamele flying and land somewhere far away.

It was just days before my fourteenth birthday when I came home from school and found Mommy home. I didn't think twice. She asked me what I'd like for dinner and paused, and then, as if taking another breath just like that she said, "Chamele is gone." And that's how I found out Chamele had left. Just those words as she breathed her life and went about her business. Busying herself, amongst the unfamiliar pots and pans. It was years before I would know the true story. I remember running to Chamele's room and just like Mommy said, she was gone, not even a trace. Nothing left but the lingering scent of the flower water she splashed about her twice a day. That night as I allowed myself to cry real tears, I held onto the single feather Chamele had left on my pillow. I still have it, even in what I would later learn was certain to be her greatest sorrow, she took time to remind me to find a happy place.

That day changed everything. Faith and trust became secondary to anger and blame. I found myself having trouble holding true to Chamele's words even though I knew that there was not a chance Chamele had taken Mommy's gold ring and diamond earrings, like Claire had told her and Daddy. Chamele's world was one in which one obeyed the Ten Commandments, and she proved in the act of leaving that she practiced them.

Thou shall not bear false witness. "Never snitch, that's a sin, Girlie. Do you understand? God don't like snitches." Years later, one of the last times the entire family was together, Claire came home and she was wearing Mommy's diamond earrings. The same ones she had accused Chamele of taking. Even then, no one said aloud what we all knew, and Chamele's name was forever cleared even in the silence. (Making it possible for me to find another happy place.)

It had been years since Mommy and Daddy had passed away and a long time since Claire and I had spoken, so with only days away from the eclipse, I phoned her. We agreed to meet for coffee and I was excited to remind her of all the places she might have forgotten, all the places that I could remember might be her happy places. I was determined to help her remember and guide her so that she might reach around and step out of the darkness into the light. It was a quick hello and a tense fifteen minutes of latte and espresso. As I sat back and watched her, listened to her talk, I found myself once again obeying Chamele. As I closed my eyes and let go, I excused myself and got up, turning away without even a goodbye.

I could hear Chamele whispering to me, "Go forward, just keep on going forward. Remember, Abigail, you ain't never s'ppose to go back. Going back ain't gonna change anything cause you're always going to come back to today. Remember that, sweetie. Always remember and always listen. I love you, Girlie."

We watch together, side by side
Yet your eyes and mine see differently.
The waves move, and voices are heard, words,
We listen, but hear differently.
Our hands rest on one another's or not.
We speak but do not hear the words as they leave
our mouths.
We remember:
We sat side by side,
we watched,
we listened,
we spoke,
Yet we remembered differently.
Does that make one of us wrong?

FADING FROST

Fading Frost

It was spring of 1934 when Martin Owings applied to study at the School of Architecture, Chicago. He was touring the campus and buildings when he saw a stack of crumpled drawings in one of the trash receptacles. Scanning the tour group and guide to make certain no one noticed, he bent down to tie his shoe. Then just as everyone headed into the hall, the guide looked back and motioned to him. He called out, he'd be right there. Once they were out of sight, he grabbed the papers.

Martin was excited to get home and flatten out the wadded papers he had stuffed in his pocket. He had indeed found something wonderful: the doodles of plans for apartments and high rises—some with steel columns; artists' visions thrown away for his taking. Martin later used several of those doodles to his advantage when designing and engineering work of his own. His professors took notice and when Ludwig Mies came to Chicago, they were happy to introduce Martin to him. Martin was thrilled when he soon became a student of Mies. And was proud of himself at having the foresight to learn German. Martin and Mies were able to communicate fluently in a way the other students couldn't and it wasn't long before Mies chose Martin to be his protégé.

Sylvia was kind, well-versed, had a beautiful smile, and she was fluent in German; Mies couldn't have been happier when she applied as a secretary in his office. She often flirted with Martin when he and Mies were meeting. She was surprised that he was not a football player or athlete, as he was a large and well-proportioned man, with big hands and soft eyes. And he flirted back; she liked that. Sometimes he would tell her a funny joke in German, whispering as if it was only for her. Often when Martin met with Mies, he would bring Sylvia chocolates or biscuits. One day, he brought her flowers and asked her to join him for dinner. She blushed and accepted his invitation and six months later, his hand in marriage. It was at their wedding that Ludwig Mies met Herbert Greenwald for the first time and it was this connection that truly put Mies on the map in creating Chicago's beautiful skyscraper. Certainly, this introduction helped in securing Martin an incredible new project in which he was made lead architect and project manager. A project, which provided him the financial freedom to do almost anything he chose, including the purchase of a house on prestigious Sheridan Road in Winnetka, overlooking Lake Michigan. And with this financial freedom, Martin began to feel the power that came with it.

He despised that Sylvia continued working and wanted her to stay at home, decorating their beautiful house and preparing dinner parties, joining women's groups and going to business functions with him. Sylvia was a strong woman—not one to stay leashed—and she loved her job. She loved meeting the new students and gifted architects who came to visit. So Martin began doing what he knew would make her change her mind. He began talking about starting a family. And he was right, Sylvia was delighted at the prospect of being a mother, and couldn't have been happier that Martin was especially anxious. Her own desires made her blind to what he was doing and so she believed him—or at least wanted to. When she happily discovered that she was pregnant, she resigned her job, promising Mies that she was there for emergencies and would someday be back.

Martin loved the social life that came with his prestigious new position and he was proud of how well Sylvia fit into her new role as his wife. She seemed to have no trouble being trained to obey his demands, as he showered her, and her growing belly, with compliments and gifts. Martin had also become a bit of a drinker and although pregnant, Sylvia enjoyed a glass of wine or a Martini when entertaining or being entertained.

When Jeffrey was born, it was the celebration of a king. Martin was the only boy in a family of seven; his father was also the only boy in a family of seven. Sylvia had five sisters; her father had been the only boy in a family of ten. There could not have been greater excitement to have a boy in the family, especially since all the other grandchildren to date had been girls. In the beginning, Sylvia loved being a mom. As excited as Martin was, he was also a bit distant; he was a proud father with little interaction. Sylvia gloated over Jeffrey and on occasion, Martin made it clear that he was still number one. And while Martin's career continued to blossom, so did the purchases not only for the house and Sylvia, but for Jeffrey as well. No one in the Owings household was void of wants or needs. Jeffrey was almost three when Sylvia became pregnant again. She was delighted and Martin was once again the beaming expectant daddy. At this point, he had become a partner at one of the largest architectural firms in Chicago, and his late night social schedule was easy to explain. When Megan was born, the celebration was a bit quieter but certainly not any less exciting. Martin loved his beautiful baby girl and made certain that she had the best of everything a princess might want. Jeffrey was the one who guaranteed the Owings name would be carried on, but it was Megan who was the apple of Martin's eye.

Sylvia made certain to introduce her children to all the arts and music. Both children excelled in art and prose and at Martin's encouragement, Jeffrey was enrolled in almost every sports program until he decided which one he liked the best. Sylvia had hoped for the little girl who loved tea parties and dress up, but Megan was a bit of the tomboy and loved experimenting with paint and water and crayons—never minding how dirty she got.

Sylvia loved helping in the children's classrooms as a room mom and was the perfect Brownie and Cub Scout leader. She did her best to arrange outings and father/daughter dances and the pinewood derby car races when Martin could attend, however he inevitably was too busy and either Sylvia would have to step in or Megan and Jeffrey would have to go with a friend and their dad. It wasn't unusual for Martin to come home a wee bit intoxicated and on several occasions, Sylvia would have a few too many. Megan and Jeffrey grew up all too familiar with the bickering of their parents, although rarely being able to understand the discussion behind it. They had each other and although had spats of their own, they loved hanging out at home together.

As they got older, Megan would attend Jeffrey's football games and Jeffrey would praise Megan's latest work of art, oftentimes critiquing it and making a suggestion or two. Jeffrey's football was Martin's joy. There wasn't anything that Jeffrey could do wrong, especially when he received a full football scholarship to the University of Michigan. Now his son would be a quarterback, at the #1 Big 10. He had been a good son, never causing any trouble. That was what Martin believed because he was never around enough to know any different. Jeffrey's accolades hung on his father's office wall and held prominent spots in framed photos on his desk. Every sports photo, trophy, and newspaper article, but nothing about his academic success.

Jeffrey wondered if his dad even knew that he had maintained a 4.0 GPA, including honors classes in history and English, and that he had decided to take the last semester off as he had enough credits to earn his diploma. It was his mom whom he knew was proud beyond belief. She, after all, had been the one to go to all his games, even away games when she could, but also enjoyed it if he shared an English paper or history essay. She was always there for Megan, too. She made sure that Megan knew how equally proud she was of all of her accomplishments, her paintings, etchings, drawings, and the personal poems. She was careful not to let her husband know that there was more to life than just money or who knew whom. She was smart enough that she didn't want herself or the children to lose that.

❄ Friends ❄

When Megan and Allison met, they could not have been a more unlikely duo. Megan cared less about what people thought of her and more about perfecting the color green. She had, in fact, developed an obsession with the vibrancy of the egg tempura technique, which was introduced loudly during the Renaissance.

She wore whatever she could grab in the morning, but it had to be something that had been her Popo's. (Her mother's dad) When he passed away, Megan took all of his shirts, sweaters, and socks, claiming them as her own. She had shared the argyle socks with her older brother, just because she was sure that would have been her Popo's wishes and she could always borrow them if she really wanted. She had the perfect metabolism and never had to worry about what went in her mouth. She prided herself on being au natural and after a month of wearing the bra her mom proudly took her to be fitted in, she stashed it in the far back of her underwear drawer. She hated that she was the first to get her period when she was ten, but loved it when she learned it meant she could get out of gym for a week every month. She had let her hair grow for years and didn't care if braids were or weren't in style, especially when she hadn't had a chance to wash it. Megan was the baby of the family but seemed to have the oldest soul. It was often she who took care of everyone else. She had a natural talent and made painting seem effortless. She painted with such realism that sometimes her paintings were mistaken for photographs.

Allison was two years older than Megan but her lack of self-confidence made her seem younger. She would never leave the house without a full face of makeup, which without a doubt accentuated her already beautiful features, including her striking blue eyes. She worried about everything she put in her mouth and counted every calorie. Allison spent hours trying to make her hair look less nappy and hated that she had inherited that trait from her father. She wore only name-brand clothes and wouldn't be caught dead in anything that might resemble a hand-me-down—unless of course it was an original Biba or Courrèges that her mom might have been lucky enough to bring home after a photo shoot.

When Allison started at New Trier High School, the football captain and team quarterback became her obsession. Although she was more artistic than athletic, she made up her mind and worked hard to make the varsity cheerleading squad, hoping he'd notice her. But as good as she was at accomplishing anything she put her mind to, she failed there. She also had a hard time when it came to time management, prioritizing, and organizing what it was she really needed in order to be true to herself. Allison knew that finding time to expand her techniques in art class was so important. She knew that ultimately it would be art that would bring her success but for now, she struggled since that wasn't interesting to the "popular" kids. In art class, she was special unto herself. Allison's work was unique; her art teacher would often refer to her work as Frank Bowling meets Grandma Moses. She usually painted with her eyes closed, which intrigued Megan since she had a difficult time painting anything that she wasn't looking at or didn't have a photograph of. Allison couldn't have been happier when she realized the varsity football captain was Megan's brother and that having Megan as a friend might play to her advantage in more ways than one. It was the beginning of a friendship that in years to come would change both girls forever.

It wasn't long after they met at the North Shore Art League that

Allison and Megan began spending more time together. Allison was less interested in cheerleading and popularity, and more interested in brush strokes and E.E. Cummings, Jeffrey's favorite poet. Allison loved spending time at Megan's because there she never felt pressured into being anyone she wasn't, especially since the word perfection wasn't even in Megan's vocabulary. They could share secrets, they could laugh until they cried, or snorted, whichever came first. Allison loved brushing the knots out of Megan's hair and braiding it when Megan didn't want to. She loved when Jeffrey would spend time with them discussing the latest music, or artist, and sometimes even the locker room gossip; she liked that he was comfortable with her that way.

❈ Brotherly Love ❈

Jeffrey and Megan had always been close; they had more in common than they wanted to admit. Both were open about the love they had had for Popo and for each other. Jeffrey envied Megan's artistic talents, but not as much as he envied her tremendous self-esteem. She was always true to herself and while she definitely knew how to have fun, she never caved to peer pressure, which meant limited social activities and friends. He, on the other hand, had an image to keep and in doing so, tried not to ever alter it, even at home. Sometimes he found that difficult, especially when Allison was around, and increasingly so when Megan started New Trier, too.

Jeffrey secretly liked Allison and was grateful for the relationship she and Megan had. When she was around, he never minded her flirting and had no problem acknowledging this younger classman at school. In fact, at Megan's begging, he took Allison to her Junior Prom. Prom was right before his last semester and Megan had waited up all night for them to come home. Allison was sleeping over and she knew Jeffrey would be shy with details. It was like having a sister and brother sometimes, and Megan loved that.

❋ The Incident ❋

It was cold out, a bitter Chicago January. Sylvia had gone to Indiana to spend a week with her mother and sister, Shelley. She wasn't worried. Jeffrey and Megan were capable of taking care of each other and Martin would after all be around. She was looking forward to some time away and Martin had a business dinner scheduled that for once didn't include wives. It would be a good time to go and maybe Martin would have a bit of time to bond with Megan and Jeffrey if she was out of the picture. She could hope. She had been told that it had been a quiet night; Allison had come over before Martin left for his dinner and she was going to spend the night. Martin liked Allison, something about her made him laugh so he didn't mind the extra body in the house. Jeffrey had decided to stay in all week and just hang out with Megan and Allison if she was there. He was excited to have no commitments and no obligations. He had been planning the night for a while. He had gotten his hands on some mushrooms and a nickel bag of pot. He was sure that Megan and Allison would think it was cool to hang out and experiment with him and he was right. They waited for Martin to leave and started smoking. It wasn't long before the munchies hit and Jeffrey thought it would be the perfect time to try the mushrooms. They were tough and bitter and hard to get down; it didn't help when Megan left and came back, she closed the door behind her, always thinking. She had a jar of peanut butter and a loaf of Wonder bread, her favorite go-to treat. Between laughing and choking, they were dying of thirst. Jeffrey opened the door and left the room, only to return with a bottle of vodka he had grabbed out of the liquor cabinet in his father's study. He forgot and left the door open; they drank and smoked some more. Their laughter became uncontrollable until they all lay on the floor and couldn't do anything but laugh. Someone, Allison or Megan or Jeffrey or all of them decided it would be a great idea to play strip poker, followed by a game of dare.

At this point, no one had any clothes on, except for Jeffrey who still had on a pair of Popo's argyle socks. The first dare was for each of them to cut their hair. Megan didn't hesitate and used the X-acto knife she had on her desk to cut off chunks at a time until her head was cropped to a generous two to three inches overall with straggling longer locks on the top and in the back. Allison didn't know if she should laugh or cry as she looked at her friend and followed suit. Jeffrey, who was just beginning to grow his hair out, wasn't too thrilled when Allison jumped in to help. The piles of hair on the floor were a mess and the artist in Allison, despite her state of mind, began picking up strands of hair and braiding them together, tying a bracelet on to each of their wrists. Bracelets that were made from combinations of all of their shredded locks. Laughter and tears followed with touching and admiring, so it was no surprise that the following dares involved sexual positions. Allison touching herself and then Megan, putting her finger gently into her and pulling in and out. Megan kissing Allison, Jeffrey wrapping himself around Allison who delighted in the touch of his naked body next to hers. Megan touching Jeffrey, which didn't go well when they realized what they were doing to whom. Jeffrey sat on Megan's bed, his back leaning against the wall. He held Allison between his legs as she leaned back against him, his hands covering her breasts. Megan took the dare and placed her head between Allison's legs and carefully began licking her vagina and moving her tongue gently and quickly as she found her clitoris. Allison arched her back and lovingly laid her hands on Megan's shoulders. Jeffrey was lost in the moment. It was a moment of pure love when Megan's head was yanked back so hard that she thought she heard a crack. Allison screamed. Jeffrey couldn't move fast enough as Megan grabbed onto his feet to hold on but instead, both socks came off in her hands. She could feel something trickle down her face, she spat and blood went everywhere.

Martin had a firm grip and grabbing the blanket that had fallen on the floor, he wrapped Megan in it like a piece of garbage waiting to go out to the trash. Her thrashing was no match for his overpowering strength. By the time Jeffrey was able to get up to help, Martin was dragging Megan on the floor, oblivious to her screams. Jeffrey grabbed him from behind and Martin turned, fist raised, and knocked Jeffrey across the jaw, causing him to stumble and fall backwards. Allison continued to scream. Megan could feel herself being dragged and pulled, petrified as her body hit the stairs, one after another. It was muffled but she could hear her dad huffing and could hear Allison scream, until there was cold and silence.

Martin lifted the rolled-up blanket with Megan still inside and threw it in the backseat of the car. Megan afraid, stayed silent and still. She must have fallen asleep because when she woke up, the car was stopped. She was able to squiggle her way out of the blanket and sat up. There in the headlights was Martin with his hands on his head, looking at the front of the car. Along the side of the road lay what appeared to be a freshly killed deer. The road was dark, so Megan wasn't sure, but nothing looked even remotely familiar. Martin angrily kicked the car and got back in. Megan was still sitting up, but thought better than to say anything. Martin looked at her more blankly than anything else and continued driving. The sun was just beginning to rise and Megan had no idea how long she had slept or where they were until she saw a road sign: "Traverse City State Hospital 5 miles" She trembled, not sure if she was more afraid of the possibility or more afraid of opening her mouth and having words come out.

Quietly she spoke, "Dad," a little louder, "Daddy, I'm sorry." He slammed on the brakes and when he turned around, his face was so red, Megan didn't recognize him.

"Sorry. Sorry, you little whore! You're nothing! You're nothing, do you understand? NOTHING!!! You have no daddy! You have NOTHING!!!!"

Megan tried hard to control herself, but she couldn't hold back. She vomited all over herself and the backseat. Martin sped up. The next time he stopped was at the front entrance of Traverse City State Hospital, where he opened the back door and pulled Megan out, wrapping the blanket around her naked body as she clung for dear life onto the socks she had pulled off Jeffrey's feet.

❊ Institution ❊

Megan remembered how she was taken from her dad despite her kicking and screaming as he did nothing. They took her away as he was escorted into an office. That was the last time she saw him.

She remembered someone giving her a shot and nothing until the next morning, when she was in some sort of operating room. She heard words, whispers, something about her dad signing a release. She felt the cold liquid on her abdomen as she was being scrubbed down. She tried to fight the balloon-like mask over her mouth and nose, without any luck. She wasn't sure how many days later she was awake and aware enough to know the devastating outcome of the reason she was left with a twelve-inch scar across her stomach. Her father had signed papers for her to have a complete hysterectomy, something the hospital highly recommended for girls her age, because it "made things so much easier." And now here she lay alone, afraid, and without answers. At least she remembered thinking someone was kind enough to leave her the argyle socks, which she now squeezed in her strapped-down hands.

That someone was Bess, a black girl not much older than Megan. She was kind and funny and had enough compassion to fill the universe. Bess' dad was a janitor at Traverse City and he had been bringing Bess along whenever he could to help cheer up the younger patients. Now Bess was in college, but still visited on occasion. She was especially anxious to meet Megan after her dad had come home talking about the newest and saddest patient yet.

"There's something special about this one," he had told his family at dinner one night. "Yes, sir, she couldn't have done anything but just once to get her brung in. Heard her own daddy did it… just up and left her there."

Bess tried to bring Megan comfort, thinking like Megan that any day she'd be released. But that first month, Megan really began to understand and learn what it took to survive. There was no tolerance of screaming, or asking questions—both brought about different punishments. Screaming put her in bed, hands and feet tied to the metal frame, while wet sheets layered with ice were laid below her and over her. When they dried, the sheets felt like rough sandpaper and would cut into her skin if she moved. Asking questions were not tolerated at all and brought her a full day of isolation in a darkened room the size of a closet. She couldn't hear or see anything and no one even came to bring her food or water all day. She was given an empty bucket and that was where she was to relieve herself, not even water to clean her hands and only four rough, brown paper towels to use for wiping.

It was here in the isolation room that Megan would come to understand the art of her dear friend Allison and her ability to see, to create with her eyes closed. Megan would remember this and find it a welcome escape whenever she could. Her heart hurt for the memories of her and Allison and also she worried. Was there some awful reason Allison had learned to paint that way? Megan only had to experience each of these punishments once to realize the extent of their effects. It was with this understanding that Megan ceased talking in front of anyone, except sometimes Bess. She practiced using her voice when on rare occasions she was alone in the shower, or in bed without being watched, as she was afraid if she didn't, she might lose her voice altogether.

Megan learned to understand the significance of Saturdays. Saturdays were mail days; everyone would wait anxiously for a letter, a bit of excitement, a glimmer of hope. Megan never got anything. She was alone with her memories and her argyle socks. Saturdays were also familiar food days. Perhaps a bowl of oatmeal or a grilled cheese sandwich, or on rare occasions brownies and ice cream. Not the non-descript mush that was usually served. Saturdays were the day before Sunday. Sundays were visitor days, which meant that Saturdays would be most current and remembered so there was nothing bad to talk about (at least that was the plan). There was no communication with anyone, unless they first contacted you. All letters had to be dictated through staff as writing utensils were prohibited. Several years earlier, a young girl had used the point of a pencil to protect herself and she had stabbed the orderly in the jugular and killed him. On Sunday mornings, after Bess went to church, she'd come with her dad and wait with Megan. Together, they would watch through the bars on the windows, hoping a visitor would come for her. But after the first month, both girls were certain it wasn't going to happen. Megan could understand her father not coming, but she didn't understand where her mom or Jeffrey were. She feared the worst. Perhaps they did not even know where she was.

The fear of the night visitors lay heavy on her as she witnessed rapes of some of the younger girls. When her stitches were removed and her scar had healed, she was afraid for herself, with good reason. She, too, had been visited—her hair played with, her vagina rubbed, rough hands on her nipples and the pulling so hard they bled, the heavy breathing and the cackle. The pain as he climbed on top and shoved himself inside. Never once did she move, never once did she open her eyes, and never once did she tell, not even Bess. But Bess knew and was helpless, fearing if she said anything at all Megan wouldn't have even her visits.

As the months grew longer, they became years. Megan kept to herself more, always wearing Jeffrey's argyle socks on her hands. She had actually worn holes for her fingers to come through; no one called her Megan any more—they called her Argyle. It seemed fitting and she liked the familiarity of the word. Bess had transferred to a school out of state and wasn't able to visit as often. Megan rarely used her voice and learned to get through most of the day with her eyes closed. Her practice for survival appeared to those around her as an act of insanity and she was treated as such. Megan wasn't sure any more if it was the lack of communication, missing her mom and brother, and Allison so much, or if it was the refusal to let her create that was the most difficult. Knowing she had to do something or she really might go crazy, she got creative. She would hoard and hide sheets of toilet paper, the two-ply kind they put out on Sundays. At night in bed, she would carefully separate the sheets. She had discovered that she could use strands of her hair to create pictures or write prose, by using the hair as thread and sewing it onto the sheets of toilet paper. She had discovered by using minuscule amounts of earwax on the tip of each strand of hair, it acted as a needle and allowed her the ability to really sew. As time went by, the poems got longer and the pictures more detailed. She began brushing random people's hair. No one knew why and because she didn't speak, no one seemed to mind. She was gentle and it was almost sensual the way she brushed one's hair. Sometimes staff and residents sought her out to get theirs brushed, even visitors sometimes didn't mind. She was a bit choosy though; she loved redheads and those with different shades of gray. They had to have hair long enough to sew without too much piecing, so long hair was so much better than short. The textures were helpful, so those with nappy hair like Bess and Allison was good too, although Megan found it much harder to brush. She would hide under her sheets and clean the brush at night; she'd separate the colors and textures as best she could. She hid the hair and the finished sheets, and carefully placed them in the hole she had made in the bottom of her mattress. Sometimes she would bite off her nails when they got long and save them in hopes that she might figure out a way to use them to draw with someday, if she was able to get her hands on some sort of color. At one point over the years, she resorted to cutting herself and using her own blood to create paintings, but she had a problem with blood soaking into the paper and everything running together, making an ugly mess. She signed each sheet with the words "May Day," hoping beyond hope that they would be found and someone might understand and look for the artist.

Megan hadn't really realized how many days, weeks, months, even years passed until she heard she was being moved. She was now officially an adult and at twenty-one, was no longer allowed to stay in the youth building. She would rock back and forth on her bed, morning and night. They would have to force her to go to the dining hall to eat where she would stuff the mush into her mouth with her fingers so she could hurry back to her bed. She was so grateful when that night Bess showed up. She had been crying, Megan knew that. They held each other, Megan holding on for dear life. Bess stroked her hair, and whispered to her, "Sweetie, I have to say goodbye. My pappy died last week and they won't let me visit you anymore. I am so sorry..." She talked through silent tears. "You know you will always be here in my heart." Bess tapped her chest. "I will get you out of here someday. Someday, I'll be back..." Megan pulled away and reached under the bed, pulling out hundreds of sheets of toilet paper, each with a poem or a picture, each one more detailed than the one before. Megan handed them to Bess and whispered, "Please take them, find them a home and maybe someone will find me. They'll know who I am. Or hang on to them for me, until you come back. Whatever you think best, but please, please don't forget me." Both girls fought back tears. Bess carefully put them in her purse and walked away.

When she got home, she sat down at the kitchen table, thinking that maybe it was a bad dream and her pappy would join her. But she knew better and she carefully pulled the sheets out, laying them on the table in front of her. She couldn't believe the detail. She found one of herself and her pappy, and examined it. It was as if someone had taken a photograph and embroidered over it to give it texture; it had indeed found its home.

The poems were surprisingly not all dark and lonely. Megan had written of flowers growing and reaching for the sun, of life inside, of her waiting to explode, and of bitterness and sorrow at the jail in which her body but not her soul was being held. The May Day signature screamed and Bess could almost hear Megan whispering those words over and over.

❈ The House ❈

Jeffrey's right side of his face began to show black and green from where his dad had hit him. He fingered the bracelet of Megan's hair still on his left wrist. He held it to his nose and breathed it in, breathed her in. Allison had gone home and he sat alone in the cold on the front steps. He sat there all night and into the early morning, knowing that at some point they would have to come home. Unintentionally, he had allowed himself to fall asleep and awoke to the sound of tires as they plowed through the leftover snow, the crispness of the sound bringing him hope. It was indeed a new day. Jeffrey stood up as his father's car pulled into the garage. Jeffrey stood at the door, seeing the dented fender and the remnants of what looked like hair and blood. He ran barefoot to meet them, but his father didn't stop until he was parked inside. Jeffrey didn't see Megan.

Martin got out of the car looking like an old man on a mission. He immediately got a bucket of water and some rags. He looked at Jeffrey. "Are you going to stand there or help? Seems to me you'd want to do something." Jeffrey didn't move as Martin continued to gather cleaning supplies. He sprayed some soap on the fender and let it soak while he walked around to the back door. He opened it and Jeffrey could smell the vomit and gagged. Martin didn't seem to notice and began to scrub. He got the Shop-Vac and vacuumed up the dirty powder and used the leather cleaner to scrub the seat. He grabbed a garbage bag and threw everything in it that was not attached to the car; all the while Jeffrey stood watching in disbelief.

"Where is she? Dad, where did you take Megan? Dad, where is Megan?" Martin kept working, spraying the fender over and over again and scrubbing and scrubbing. Jeffrey raised his voice to a scream, "Where is Megan, Dad?" Martin, still ignoring him, continued cleaning. Jeffrey came up from behind him and grabbed his shoulder, turning him around. With tears in his eyes now, he screamed, "Tell me what you did to her? Where is she?"

Martin stood up, looked Jeffrey straight in the eyes and said, "She's gone." Then he gathered up the garbage and the cleaning supplies, dried the fender, sprayed the inside of the car with new car deodorant, and went in the house, while Jeffrey just stood there and watched.

After several minutes, Jeffrey went inside. He went to his room and paced. He paced for what must have been hours. He watched the clock's minute hand move slowly, waiting for the hour hand to reach seven. He didn't want to call his mom too early and figured that would be an okay time. He must have fallen asleep, because it was on the ten when he awakened to the smell of bacon and pancakes cooking. He jumped off the bed, relieved; it had to have just been a nightmare. But then on his way downstairs to breakfast, he stopped at Megan's door. It was closed; he knocked quietly at first and then a bit louder before slowly opening the door. Inside, it was like the twilight zone; he had stepped into another dimension. The room was empty. Empty of everything but her desk and a bed made up with a bedspread he had never seen. It was free from any signs that it may have belonged to Megan, let alone anyone. It was clearly void of any human touch. He opened the closets, looked under the bed, in the desk drawer. Nothing, none of her hair from the night before, no canvases, or sketchbooks. No paints, nothing. It was as if she had never existed.

In the kitchen, Martin sat at the table finishing up a cup of coffee and reading the Wall Street Journal. There was a uniformed black woman at the sink, her hands wet as she finished cleaning up the dishes.

She looked up when Jeffrey walked in. Nodding, she said, "Morning, sir." Jeffrey hated that and Martin knew it. He smirked and raised his mug to his mouth. Trying hard to control himself, Jeffrey pulled the chair out next to Martin and sat down. Martin continued reading the paper.

"Ok, so I screwed up." Before he could say anything else, Martin slammed down the paper and stood up. He went to over to the sink, put some money in the woman's hand, and quietly whispered something to her that Jeffrey couldn't hear. She wiped her hands on her apron, said goodbye, and quickly and quietly left. Martin waited until she was gone and turned around to face his son.

"Screwed up? Don't talk to me about screwing up. You start school in less than six months. There is no screwing up, do you understand?" Jeffrey stood up and approached his dad.

"Where is Megan, Dad? What did you do to Megan?!" Martin turned towards the sink and he grabbed a knife from the counter. When he turned back again, his face was red and he didn't even look like himself. He raised the knife, stopping himself just short of Jeffrey. He slammed it down, hard enough for it to stick straight up.

"Look at that! Remember the damage it can do, and don't ever mention that name again. Not in front of me. Not in this house. Not anywhere! Do you understand? There is NO MEGAN. She NEVER was!!!!!" Martin pulled the knife out of the countertop for effect, raised it for show, and then slammed it in again before leaving the kitchen and the house.

Jeffrey was thrown by the entire series of events. He was afraid for himself, but mostly for his sister and how was he going to tell his mom. He knew he had to call her. She would need to come home; she would get to the bottom of this and Megan would be home soon. He called Allison first, with Megan gone, he needed to reach out—he needed Allison to know how he felt. In an instant, everything could change and he didn't want to lose Allison. He played with the braided bracelet of Megan's hair as they spoke, but they were soon interrupted by her mom. Allison and Jeffrey had spoken just long enough for Allison to tell him that her parents had been contacted by Martin and she wasn't going to be able to see him anymore.

Allison's mom broke in, "Jeffrey, I'm so sorry, but Allison can't talk to you again," and then the phone went dead. Jeffrey allowed himself to cry and he sobbed as he looked through the papers on his desk for the information Sylvia had left on where she was staying. He pushed the buttons on the phone and called.

The front desk receptionist tried the room, but after there was no answer, she came back on. "I'm sorry, sir. It seems that they are not in the room. Would you care to leave a message?" Trying not to sound too desperate, he left a message for Sylvia Owings to call home.

The sun was already setting and Martin was back home, a new car in the garage, when she finally called. Jeffrey rushed to answer the phone that he had been waiting all day to ring, but Martin with a drink in his hand and several already consumed, beat him to it. Jeffrey listened, not sure if he should interrupt, as he heard his dad say, "Sylvia sweetie, everything is wonderful here. The kids and I are having a wonderful time. I'm not sure why you would have gotten a message to call home. No, actually Jeffrey took Megan and Allison to a movie. They should be home in a bit... just have a great time and I'll tell the kids you called. Send my love to your mom and Shelley. See you soon. Bye." Jeffrey heard the phone slam and grabbed his coat to leave as he heard Martin coming up the stairs. He tried to make it down the back staircase when Martin grabbed him from behind. He was careful not to do too much damage, but just enough to send Jeffrey a message.

As the blood ran down Jeffrey's face from a cut when Martin slammed his head against the wall, Martin said, "You didn't get the message? Now you do!" Jeffrey didn't know where to go or what to do, He couldn't leave, not before his mom got home. He went back in his room and slammed the door.

Sylvia hung up with Martin and said her goodbyes to her mom and sister, explaining a bit desperately, "I need to go home. I'm sorry. We'll do it again soon, I promise." There was something in his tone—she'd heard it too many times before—that slurred speech when he'd had a bit too much to drink. That arrogant tone, the one that said, "Leave me alone. I don't need you." But it was the "Jeffrey took Megan and Allison to a movie, they should be home in a bit," that sent the red flag. Martin would never let Jeffrey use his car, his precious Cadillac, and Sylvia was driving the Chevy. The drive home was excruciatingly long. The intuition only a mother knows was pulling at her; something was desperately wrong. The weather was bad and traffic slowed to a standstill. Sylvia put the window down and welcomed the coolness of the wet wind against her face; wet snow blew into the car and she could feel it melting on her lap. It was a welcome diversion. Her heart ached to get home.

She arrived just before dinner, hoping they hadn't eaten yet. She pulled into the garage and immediately noticed something was off. The house was dark and she found Martin sitting in his study, a drink in one hand and a bottle in the other. It was quiet, too quiet. She walked over to him before he even heard her coming. She knew it would be a mistake; she just didn't know how big. He dropped the glass and raised the bottle, liquor spilling out. He was about to smash it into someone when she said, "Whoa, that's some welcome home."

Martin's face was blank for a minute until he brought himself back to the moment and the reality that his wife was home. "Good thing I didn't hit you with this," he said as he raised the bottle in her direction. "Might have knocked you out." He put his arms around her to welcome her home. "So you're home early."

"Yep, just thought I might be needed here," she said, looking around. "Where are Jeffrey and Megan? It's so quiet."

"He's in his room." Martin raised his eyes towards the ceiling.

"And Megan, where's she?" Martin threw the glass across the room. "What is this, an interrogation? How the hell should I know? She's gone."

"Gone?" Sylvia knew the man who stood in front of her all too well. She needed to keep her composure. For years, she had been living in a shadow, walking on eggshells, understanding as a woman and wife of such a powerful and successful man what was at stake. "Martin, where did she go?"

"How the fuck should I know? She's gone and she's not coming back. Do you understand me, Sylvia? She's not ever allowed to come back." Holding back tears, Sylvia left and made her way into the hall before he grabbed her. That was when Jeffrey heard the commotion and came downstairs. There was a lot of screaming; Jeffrey tried getting between them, and Sylvia made her way free and unthinking, dialed 911.

It wasn't long before the police arrived; after all, Martin was well known in the community and the Sheridan Road address warranted priority status. The security camera beeped as the unidentified cars pulled in and Martin stepped outside the door to meet them. His hair was a bit tousled and he smelled of booze, but he was presentable and cordial. With a sense of humor, he explained, "Jeffrey, you know he was the winning quarterback at homecoming? Well, we were wrestling around when my wife came home, surprised the shit out of us. She wasn't supposed to be back for another couple of days, and well, you know women. She saw us wrestling about and didn't even ask. Can you imagine didn't even say "hi?" Just called you."

They laughed, chatted a bit more, discussed the storm coming, asked once more that all was well just because it was their job, and then said, "Have a great night, Mr. Owings. And best to your son."

Martin went back inside, slamming the door. Sylvia and Jeffrey had already gone upstairs, and so his rant was unheard. He went back into the den and continued drinking. Jeffrey and Sylvia sat in Megan's room, Sylvia wanting to see what she might find and wanting, no needing, to feel her daughter's presence. She needed to remain stoic. She knew Martin—he was stubborn and when angry, a bit frightening. All too often, she had protected herself and her children by remaining strong and keeping her emotions in check. Jeffrey retold the events to the best of his recollection. Sylvia asked him several times to repeat what time Martin left and the time he returned home. She attempted to calculate distance; she knew Martin didn't have it in him to kill her, so she had to figure out where he'd leave her. He might have hurt her, that would not surprise her. After all, she had her own memories and scars of his temper-induced outbursts. Jeffrey kept trying, apologizing for his time lapse, apologizing for getting them into this. He had a hard time holding it together and Sylvia knew Jeffrey just wanted Megan home. Sylvia took Jeffrey's hand and put her fingers on the braided bracelet. She held it to her nose, smelling her daughter, and uncharacteristically let a tear roll down her cheek.

❈ Searching ❈

Sylvia had convinced Jeffrey to start school early. He had thought about not going altogether, but realized that was not a viable option given Martin's volatility. So instead, he listened to his mom and decided it was better for him to get away from the house than to wait around for graduation. He'd contacted the coach and made plans to leave. He attempted to reach Allison again; he felt so empty now with Megan missing and Allison forbidden to see him. But the number had been disconnected and when he drove past the house, it was dark and someone had put a "For Sale" sign out on the front lawn. He couldn't imagine how they had moved so quickly, but of course, it must have had to do with his dad. Martin could buy anyone off; he was proud of that.

Sylvia and Jeffrey went alone to move him to school. They had purposely picked a time when Martin would be unable to go. When Sylvia returned, she immediately played the game, the one she had been playing for years. Making Martin think she was his puppet, pretending to be happy and obedient while she did everything she could to be comfortable, to survive, and to assure that her children would never be in want of anything. The trick was to make any idea Martin's, to make all the discussions his instigation. She continuously tried to get Martin to open up, to slip up and say something, anything about Megan and where she might be. But when Martin wouldn't answer any of her questions and instead, would grab a drink, or reach out to grab her, or scream at her, sometimes just random yelling, she decided she had had enough and she moved into Megan's room. She'd spend nights going over every little detail Jeffrey had told her, praying something had been left behind or left out. She tried to picture that night, tried to see it through Megan's eyes. She went on day trips that would take her within an eight-hour radius to her destinations and back. She drove every square foot, stopped at every gas station and restaurant along the route. She searched the libraries and the hospitals. She went to small-town police stations, begging them to acknowledge her. She carried Megan's picture everywhere, asking person after person if they might have seen her.

In the early days, Martin would come into her at night and she'd get up and go back into their room; something about being with him in Megan's room for obvious reasons didn't work. But when giving him what he wanted and satisfying his every whim didn't get her even a small clue, she got sick of his smell, his oversized belly, the way he looked, and the person he was; she got sick of him. She got in the habit of telling him she was sick, or pretending to be asleep. She knew that would turn him off.

It was on what would have been Megan's sixteenth birthday that Sylvia realized how to hurt Martin the most. She went and bought a brand new 1970 Triumph TR6 for thirty-five hundred dollars and found a young girl to give it to. Just like that, poof, it was gone and so was the money. Money was all Martin cared about and so it was money Sylvia began to take and give away. Every year on Megan's birthday, every holiday, Sylvia would buy a big-ticket item and then find someone to give it to. She opened a savings account in her own name with Jeffrey as the beneficiary. She would transfer money sporadically to her account and she would take extra cash to pay for groceries, or gas or having her hair done. She would take what she could when she could and on a regular basis, made sure that Martin sent money to Jeffrey and insisted that if Megan was indeed alive as he protested she was, that an equal amount of money be set aside for her as well. Martin didn't argue for fear that she might leave, causing a scandal. He insisted that when anyone asked, they share the wonderful news that they had sent Megan to Europe to study with the masters. No, his life had to appear perfect and in order.

Years later, he didn't much care what she wanted and would push her awake and force himself on her, never caring if she bled or cried, only concerned that he was satisfied. From the very beginning, Sylvia placed ads in the personals in newspapers around the country. Each year, she'd renew them. She was always watching over her shoulder, always looking in the faces of girls on the street. When they were out of town, even out of the country, she'd be looking for signs of Megan. She always knew that somewhere Megan was out there, confused and wondering why her mom didn't come for her. She grew closer to Jeffrey and welcomed his various girlfriends into her life, but there was a void that no one but Megan could fill and a wall that she had built between her and Martin that was almost complete. As the money in her accounts grew, the wall became stronger. Someday, she'd bring him down; someday, he'd have to answer or die paying.

❋ Watching ❋

Martin and Jeffrey had stopped communicating completely after the police incident and once Jeffrey was out of the house, they barely saw one another. Martin learned over time how to handle holidays alone. Jeffrey never came home once he left, not that Martin was aware. He never answered his phone or returned letters. On rare occasions when Martin would force Sylvia to let him join her on a trip to visit Jeffrey at school, he would go to watch him play in a game, but afterwards Jeffrey made himself too busy for anything but a wave. Sylvia understood, but Martin was furious.

Secretly, Sylvia and Jeffrey were most grateful for the scholarship because it meant that Martin was owed nothing, not even thanks, and therefore had no control; Jeffrey was truly free of him. Sylvia made certain of that with the money she took and the purchases she alone made. It may have been Martin's money, but it was Sylvia who knew how to spend it and how to hide it.

Martin would go back to work and gloat about his son as if life was perfect. No one could ever know how lonely he was on the holidays, or any day for that matter. And as often as Sylvia searched and pried, Martin distanced himself more and watched. He knew that no one could really trace him, but he often wondered if someone would contact Mies, after all it was his name he used when he dropped her off. His name he used to sign the papers. Surely, somewhere or sometime over the years, he imagined Megan would get through and tell them her name. Somehow, she would get out and find him. He was always watching over his shoulder, secretly fearful. So he drank, and when that didn't deaden the fear, he drank some more.

❋ Redeeming ❋

Megan's disappearance seemed to take the greatest toll on Jeffrey. He could never quite shake the guilt he felt at including her and Allison in the first place. His little sister, whom he secretly idolized more than he had ever let her know. Her ability to be herself, unafraid of what others thought, her talent, her self-esteem, her creativity, and her compassion. Like Sylvia, he believed she was out there somewhere. He hated his father, but truly didn't believe even he could go so far as to kill her. She was a fighter and no matter what, she'd survive

He spent as little time as possible at football practice, and gave just enough on the field to keep his scholarship. He threw himself into classes, focusing on pre-law and then law school, in the back of his mind thinking he'd find a way to get back at his dad, a way to force him into divulging what happened. That never seemed to happen.

His mom was his rock, always supporting him financially and emotionally. Together, they kept Megan alive.

Jeffrey continued to be popular with the girls and later women, but he was never fully committed. There was always something missing, a hole in his heart that needed to be filled. The bracelet Allison had made of Megan's braided hair he now kept in the back of his wallet since it had gotten too frayed to wear. He'd often find himself taking it out and rolling it in his fingers or holding it to his face; sometimes he'd think he could still smell the scent of Megan's shampoo or the scent of sweat from Allison's fingers. As a prosecuting attorney, he was happy to argue cases in honor of Megan: domestic abuse, women's issues, and gay rights. During high anxiety cases, he'd make sure it was in his pocket and he'd roll it gently between his fingers as he gave his closing argument.

Over the years, he attempted on several occasions to find Allison. He once heard she had been sent to school in Europe to train with the masters, but when he'd searched further, he'd always come up empty. It was into his fifth year of practicing law that he took a few months off to travel. His dad had since retired, and his mom longed for time away from him and wanted a traveling companion. It was a perfect opportunity to take a long overdue break and spend some quality time with his mom while he still could. He had moved to Wisconsin where he had attended law school and received his current position. It worked out well since he wasn't too far from home and his mom could visit as often as she liked without too much trouble. They decided on a road trip, visiting small-town art shows and big city galleries. They talked about Megan and Allison, always hoping one of the shows or galleries would turn up the jackpot. The last day of their trip took them to Southfield, Michigan. Walking down Main Street they happened upon the Park West Gallery. It was closed, but in the window were teaser prints of the current exhibit: "Bits of Megan," Meet the Artist, Monday 6-9. They stopped in their tracks, a chill passing through them. They stayed in Southfield an extra day, both knowing who the artist was.

Allison was a beautiful woman, even more so than Jeffrey had remembered. She seemed more confident, but Jeffrey could see the same emptiness in her that he felt. She was drinking a glass of wine and talking to an elderly couple when Jeffrey and Sylvia approached. She glanced up and dropped the glass, apologizing as wine splattered everywhere. Trying to make light of it, the woman kindly said, "At least it's white." Allison excused herself and didn't know who to hug first. She grabbed them both; she didn't want to ever have to let go again.

Together, they walked around the gallery. They didn't need to speak as the pictures spoke volumes. Each painting or print in the collection included somewhere small strands of braided hair. Sylvia reached out to touch them and when the curator approached, Allison shooed him away.

"She's out there, you know," she whispered, trying to catch her breath.

"Yes, we know," Sylvia and Jeffrey responded. Allison did her duty and continued to mingle for the next two hours, discussing the techniques of her work. But she never once took her eyes off Jeffrey. It had been too long. They went to dinner and without hesitation, Jeffrey proposed. Sylvia breathed a sigh of relief when Allison asked, "What took you so long?" They were married the next day at the county courthouse with Sylvia as their witness. It had been fifteen plus years since they had last seen or talked to one another, but the energy between them, the love and the conversation, picked up as if it had been yesterday. Allison was a little hesitant to explain how Martin had been paying her parents for years to keep her away; she was ashamed at their lack of pride. Sylvia didn't say much. They died last year in a car accident in southern France. Jeffrey held her and told her he was sorry, but she said she wasn't.

"If they hadn't died, truthfully, I never would have been able to complete the series and never would have come back. We never would have found each other." It was surprising how little Allison had with her, she had truly become a minimalist. Megan would have liked that. They never did see Martin, and Sylvia was depleted by the new information. She, too, was going to have a hard time going home to him.

Allison and Jeffrey settled in Wisconsin where he continued to practice and she continued to paint and create. Sylvia stayed with them more than she did at the house in Winnetka. Martin's drinking had become such that he usually didn't even notice. Allison got pregnant the first year and there was no question when their daughter was born that they would name her Megan. Sylvia wasn't sure if she liked it, but felt it wasn't her place to say. Allison welcomed the help and was happy to see Sylvia with a baby in her arms.

Martin died three years later, never having seen Allison or Jeffrey again and never once having met his granddaughter. Sylvia and Jeffrey had long discussed what would happen to the house after Martin died.

They knew that until they found Megan, there was no way that they could sell it, and so with Allison's agreement, they all moved back.

Those first nights were the hardest; ghosts seemed to wander the halls and the memories made tensions high. But it was a good house, beautiful, paid for, and renovated—Sylvia had seen to that years earlier. There was enough room that Sylvia had a wing of her own and yet helped out whenever she was needed or wanted, which was often. Pictures of Megan that Sylvia had found and hidden away now hung along the walls. Allison and Jeffrey were both happy to have her back. They had forgotten those pictures, but never her smile, the aura that surrounded her, and her unconditional love. They hoped that they would be able to tell Megan stories about her aunt that didn't include the night she disappeared. They were all sorry that all of her artwork had been destroyed or something—Martin never did say what he did with them.

Megan grew up quickly. She loved having the run of the house and the attention of everyone in it. She had the best of everything and opportunities to go along with her every possible talent. She took ballet, gymnastics, swimming, and tennis, but what she loved most was painting. Like her mom and namesake, you might have thought she was born with a paintbrush in her hand. She learned early on to paint with her eyes closed and created works that had detail similar to her aunt's. She was especially close to Sylvia and loved to share secrets with her grandma. Often, even as she reached adolescence, one could hear them giggling at wee hours of the night. It was especially hard on her when just before her thirteenth birthday, Sylvia died peacefully in her sleep, the way she would have wanted.

The emptiness of the house was often unbearable for the entire family and finding a summer and winter home seemed like perfect timing. Spending holidays in Winnetka was never an option and without Sylvia, exotic destinations didn't seem much fun. So they chose Frankfort,

Michigan, a small town on the Betsie Lake, with easy access to Lake Michigan and an artist palette with miles of trails and awesome dunes. It was a perfect distance, less than a six-hour drive. Allison had fallen in love with the lighthouse on a previous trip and she and Sylvia had always talked about buying something there. She missed that they hadn't done it prior to Sylvia's passing. She would miss her every minute and so would Megan.

Megan was surprised how much she loved it there and even with the bitter cold, she didn't mind spending time in the winter. Allison had arranged for her to go to school there in the winter and Megan had had no trouble at all making friends and fitting in. She felt like she could be an entirely different person than at New Trier. She loved how laid back it was and it didn't hurt that she had met her first love the first summer they were there—a local boy who was popular and nice and happy to bring her into the circle.

❉ Waiting ❉

The adult buildings were different, darker if that was even possible. The screaming was more constant and the number of "inmates" restrained, troublesome. There were far more people in the adult buildings that had just been left behind, or whose same-sex preference had declared them insane, and whose confinement had actually caused some of them to be just that.

Megan was an early target for the sexual advances of the orderlies and learned early on that none of them liked a dirty woman. So in addition to not speaking, Megan decided not to bathe or shower either. And if she got too fat, they didn't like her, although she didn't like that either. Too skinny and they thought maybe she wouldn't fight back. But she had figured out that by chipping her front tooth, she could use it as a weapon. The chip in it made it just sharp enough to cause pain when used on what they liked to refer to themselves as "admirers." It wasn't long before she made herself known as the one to stay away from, and for that, she was grateful.

She continued to hoard toilet paper sheets and create art, storing it in the mattress once again. When the yarn on her argyle socks became thin and frayed, she was blessed to have a nurse bring her a clean pair of socks. With supervision, she also allowed her a needle and yarn to sew the bits and pieces left on, creating a sort of patchwork socks. She also had the nurse cut out places for her fingers. It was in whispers that she communicated and gave thanks.

Over the years, there were days she would awaken, believing it all a dream. She would look out the window, hoping beyond hope that the bars were just a figment of a nightmare she was awakening from. There were sporadic visiting days when she thought she recognized someone, but then no one. She could tell by the way people dressed and the small accessories with them that they talked on that times were changing. The nurse told her they were phones. Because there were no clocks or televisions, not even radios, Megan had no true conception of reality or time or change. Her hair was graying and she had hands that were beginning to look like she remembered her grandma's. She would not allow herself to really imagine how many years she had been trapped. In the winter of 1999, she was finally able to receive a letter. It came from Bess—it had been opened so Megan wasn't sure if anything was missing. There were photographs of Bess and her children and her husband, proudly holding a grandchild in his arms. They all looked so happy; Megan remembered that feeling. The letter was a reminder that she had not been forgotten, not even after all these years. Bess mentioned that she had heard that the state hospitals were closing one at a time. She sent wishes that Traverse City would soon be one. She left a phone number and an address in Washington, D.C.; she told her that she still had all of her artwork safe in a box for when she was ready.

She ended it with, "Be well, my dear friend. You are always in my heart and always loved, Bess" Megan had emotions of joy and sorrow and read the letter and looked at the photographs so many times that she had actually worn a small hole in the paper. She couldn't help but wonder what had become of her own family. Did they think of her? Did they try to find her? Several times, she had been referred to as the "Mies girl." How would they ever find her when that wasn't even her name? She often wondered if they thought she was dead.

It was still years later when things began to change. There was less security and people were constantly coming and going. Official-looking people would walk through the halls, making notes, nodding at the "patients." Van loads of clothing came in and there were volunteers who sorted through everything, putting it in neat piles. For the first time that Megan could remember, one by one they were called into the director's office, with a security guard, nurse, and social worker present. They were asked if they understood that the hospital was closing, if they had anywhere to go, if they felt capable of functioning on the "outside." After just ten minutes or so, they were told when they could leave or would have to leave. They offered Megan the option to go to a halfway house until she could figure it out. They asked her what she thought she might need. She looked at the calendar on the wall: January 2003. She put her head in her argyle-covered hands and wept. It was the first time she had seen a date and the reality set in. It had been more than thirty years.

❈ Outside ❈

It was a difficult day when Megan was dropped off at the halfway house. One of the nurses had volunteered to drive her and get her settled. Megan was grateful for that. She wasn't quite sure what a halfway house was and not sure if she was ready to use her words or voice. She had not been out of the confines of the hospital for so long, nothing looked familiar: the cars, the restaurants, the window displays. The halfway house was above a series of stores on Main Street. She was given a key to get in at street level and another key to get into a room that would be hers. She couldn't even imagine what that would mean. The nurse parked and they went inside. It was a bit smoky in the stairwell, but the nurse informed her that smoking was prohibited so it shouldn't be too often. It was noisy too, not in the same way the hospital had been noisy, but there was music and talking, conversations. A few of the people they passed were young, like she remembered Jeffrey. They were cordial and said, "Hey." Megan put her head down, still not certain how free or safe she was.

The nurse showed her the hall bathroom and assured her that she was on the waiting list to get a room with a private bath. Megan smiled at the image. She showed her the communal kitchen, and the eight individual cabinets—each labeled with a resident's name. She opened the one labeled Mies. Megan looked at it as tears streamed down her face. Even her identity had been taken from her and now on the outside, she began to really understand.

"I'll take you shopping before I leave so we can fill it up," the nurse told Megan. They walked down the hall and she gave Megan the key to open the door. Megan had to readjust the argyle socks, her hands shaking. She pushed the door open to a bright room with a bed, a dresser, a desk, and a small television. The windows were bar-less, and the first thing Megan did was look out. The nurse told her she'd be right back and left, leaving the door open. It was the dead of winter but Megan opened the window. She felt the crispness of freedom before closing it. The nurse came back with a suitcase and two big bags. "Come on, I'll help you pretty this up," she told Megan as she took out a bright green bedspread and brand new blue sheets. "Your friend Bess sent a letter. She thought these would be your colors." Megan made a note she'd have to see about getting a phone and stamps, a way to get in touch, to say thanks. Once the bed was made and the bedspread put on, she put pillows on top, giving it a homey feeling. She folded some towels and put them in a decorative storage box next to the dresser and a bucket with toiletries. "Reminds me of my college days," the nurse smiled, and Megan could only dream of what that must have been like. "You'll take this with you when you shower or wash up. You know, whenever you need to use the facilities." Megan sort of giggled. She was known for not doing that too often, a sure way to keep away the crazies, but now that would change. The suitcase was full of clothes that had been donated. "We sort of had to guess. I hope these will fit," nurse said, holding them up before she refolded them and put them in the dresser drawers. She picked up a small flat keypad and turned on the television. It had been thirty years since Megan had watched television. She wondered if Eddie's father ever married, or if Gilligan ever got off the island. But when the nurse surfed through the channels, it was clear that time indeed was quite different now. The nurse showed her the buttons, sound, channel up, number buttons to go direct to the desired channel. "Here, you try. You'll be amazed at how many different things are on and how much there is at your disposal to learn." She tried to be nice, Megan knew that, but her blood began to boil. She had lost so much.

The nurse took her to the grocery store, an experience that was exciting and exhausting. Megan asked if there might be a library close by and found it was within walking distance of the halfway house. There was a park just outside the window where Megan could see the children and their moms passing through, almost running to avoid the cold. Megan for once didn't mind the cold. The first night alone Megan didn't sleep. She listened and she watched television. There was so much to learn, so much she had missed, and people kept mentioning 9/11. She would have to find out what that was.

There were so many smells. She sat and watched out the window, the moonlight peering through the trees, shadows dancing across the storefronts. It had been years since she had been given the opportunity to express herself. She almost wanted to open the window and scream, "I'm alive! Here I am!" But secretly, she thought perhaps she was being set up and that she would have to go back. So she remained silent, with occasional whispers.

She was surprised how quickly things came back to her. She remembered how to cook breakfast, banana French toast with peanut butter and honey. Allison and Jeffrey loved it when she made it and tasting it, she remembered why. She took a risk and asked the young girl who had just come into the kitchen to make breakfast for herself if perhaps she'd like a piece. How good it felt to have that option. Each night, she would sit and watch out the window, deciding if she had the nerve to search for her family, if they had indeed ever searched for her. She wondered how her father had lived with himself all those years, if he knew what her life had been like: a prison with no school, no books, and no art. Did he ever think of her pain? What would she say to him if she found him?

But most of all, she looked out the window and saw canvases, giant canvases on the storefront windows that each night when the moon came out were covered in Jack Frost's breath. She had been collecting twigs from the park, sharpening them into scribes. She timed everything: when the last car passed, when the last dog was walked, when the sun came up. And after several weeks at the halfway house, she knew she wasn't going back. She really was free and she decided to use the storefronts as her canvas. Their enormity was what she had missed so much, a far cry from individual sheets of toilet paper. And so in the cover of darkness, she would go outside, and using the sharpened twigs on the frosted windows, she would close her eyes and create. Elaborate scenes of her house, her family, her friends, and herself. And she would watch from her window every morning as the sun came up and melted the frost and her creation away. Long before anyone could see them in their entirety, they were gone. Until one morning when it was so cold and cloudy that the sun had not yet done its job and people stood in front of the window and talked to one another.

"Who was the artist?"

"Where did they go?"

"How could they?"

"Do you recognize that?"

"Do you know who that is?" And then slowly, the sun would rise and warm the window and the picture would simply vanish. After several such days, news people came and cameras capturing partial pictures just before they vanished altogether. There was speculation about who had done this; storeowners fought over whose window might be next and left out food and blankets. News crews set up for the night in hopes of catching the phantom artist. Megan sat in her room, watching from the window and waited for them to go away.

❉ An Adventure ❉

Frankfort was such a small town, and the local kids were always looking for something to do. The buzz was all over about some crazy artist in Traverse City who had etched into the frost of the local store windows. No one had yet to see them do it, or knew who it was. Megan and her friends were obsessed and planned to drive there and stake it out. They were determined to catch the artist in the act.

There was something about the scenes that had been captured on the news, even though they were just remnants, that Megan thought she recognized. Her parents had heard about it and read the stories but Traverse City was a drive and there was no way they were going to let Megan go with friends in the Michigan winter overnight, actually an all-nighter as she explained. So when she planned an overnight with her girlfriends, they all told each other's parents that they were staying at one another's house. Then, with the boys who had their licenses, they all drove north to camp out and watch.

Allison, having a mother's intuition moment, called the Atwells at eleven to talk to Megan, but they thought that Wendy was staying with them. Panic set in. Jeffrey and Allison quickly got in the car and made their way to Traverse City, afraid and angry. They couldn't believe that Megan had lied. It was an hour and a half before they arrived in the city and they could see a group of kids huddled together, hiding. As they drove closer, they saw Megan approaching the artist, a rendering of Allison large as life on the window.

Jeffrey pulled over and paused before getting out of the car. As he yelled "Megan," both his daughter and the artist turned around.

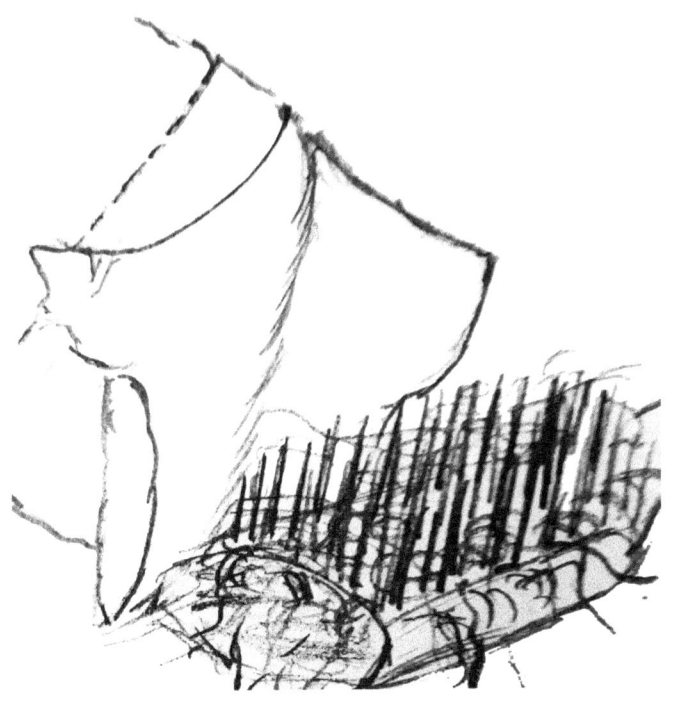

Tomorrow

A surprise package
just waiting to be torn open
To reveal it's contents
it sits in the middle of a crowded room
but no one wants to go near it.

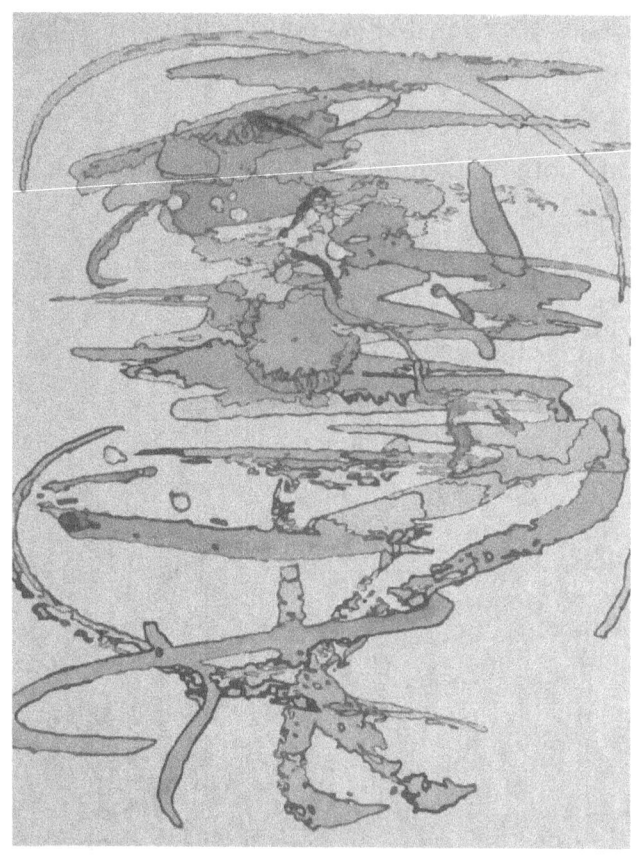

light takes over although it's night
and the crickets song
has changed
soon I hear everything in a strange new
way
A way which tells me
freedom is in the wind
the wind is in me

called upon
by none other but my own
creator
I know not
the words to plead
my life
nor can I think of a farewell
so I leave nothing said
nothing done
only my past wishes
which are now left behind.

crests of the
sun; moon
falling
on my head
splitting
in half
my forgotten
life
making it better
than before
long gone hope
my eyes (sealed shut)
see the nomads
unseeable land

only once
can I remember
the time of day, the sun shone just
above me
just out of my reach
the birds, all singing a different
song
only once
can I remember
seeing only, bright happy colors
without any at all gray,
but then
the time came when it was over
I have just memories now
the memories
which shall
never leave
my side

THE PERFECT LOAD

The Perfect Load

Over the years, it was more than just distance that separated my older sister Miranda and me. A distance that had allowed us to become satisfied if we saw each other just once a year. This seldom included any visit she made back home. It was always something about her plans and how they conveniently didn't include time with me. I guess that had something to do with how I planned my visits to her. Usually, I planned my visit to Miranda's when she seemed most needy; I suppose it was because it was the only time that I felt wanted. In actuality, it was probably just a time when I was most tolerated.

I spent more time preparing to visit Miranda than I would if I were preparing for a weeklong trip to England to visit the queen. I carefully laid out my outfits for the weekend, making certain that I had enough so that I wouldn't wear the same thing twice. I made certain to pack light enough that I wouldn't have to pay for a checked bag. Additionally, I made sure not to take my blue jeans, the pair that were a bit worn in the knee, (my favorite and most comfortable pair) and I would need to pray that the weather wasn't too hot, as I couldn't be caught dead bringing a tank top. Instead, I packed the clothes which would focus on being chic, but modest; as usual this meant a shopping trip with my eldest daughter, Kristy, to pick out my weekend wardrobe.

On my arrival, it didn't take long to realize my first mistake. I had packed my old grey slippers. Miranda didn't waste a second in commenting. "How could you wear those dirty things?" Mortified, I didn't know how to hide, since my pajama bottoms weren't long enough to cover the worn flannel that my toes pleasurably sank into. I spent the remainder of each day fully clothed until it was time to say good night and head upstairs to my niece Angela's bedroom where I would sleep.

Miranda relaxed, curled up in her madras cotton pajama bottoms and matching camisole. Her baby blue slipper socks looking uncomfortably clean. She didn't notice, I'm sure. She didn't see my discomfort after a long day of following her directions, which included restocking cabinets, the refrigerator and freezer with what appeared to be long overdue refilling. Buying refrigerated cookie dough was painful, bringing back memories of days long ago.

I remembered the day when I realized my best friend had become my big sister. My big sister whose attention I relished. I felt privileged any time I was included in cookie making, shopping, or just hanging. I looked at Miranda and wondered what had happened to cause such space, such emptiness. Somewhere between her marrying Peter and my marrying Carl, somewhere between having families of our own, somewhere in the relationships we had or didn't have with our older sisters, Megan and Laura, Miranda and I must have gotten lost, or lost something.

The vibrant Miranda I looked up to, idolized, the Miranda full of life and active was lost, too. As I thought about why I was there, I wondered how I could have missed so much. When had she really become so frail? I never understood what was wrong with her. No one seemed to know and we were never to ask, yet year after year, she became weaker, sicklier. I wondered as I worked. We had started in her bedroom; she sat on the chair directing me. I moved boxes around, in and out of her closet, rearranging. As I began pulling some of Peter's clothes down, a bit of me was not only sad and confused, but truly uncertain of what I would do and how I would feel. It hadn't been a year since Peter died unexpectedly. I don't think any of us ever really knew the cause, but I guess none of us had to. Miranda seemed at peace with it.

I thought about Carl, my husband of twenty-five years. What would I do if he suddenly dropped dead? Would I feel suddenly free and elated? Would my world crumble, or like Miranda would I move forward and simply be at peace? I kept these thoughts turning over in my mind as she continued to give direction to my task at hand.

There were so many clothes. It was evident that Peter was never one to want. Almost as if getting dirty meant just buying another shirt, suit, sweater, pants, whatever it was that had a stain here or spot there.

I looked at her pale skin, and thin lips, and felt pain. Then pushed in the corner of the closet, behind everything, I reached down and pulled out a very wrinkled light blue dress shirt. Unwadding it, I couldn't imagine that the bright red lipstick stain on Peter's collar could have been hers. In the best of times, Miranda just wasn't your bright red lipstick kind of girl. Miranda half-grimaced, half-smiled as she watched me.

I continued to put suits and dress shirts in one pile, casual clothes in another, and ties by themselves.

Before too long, both Miranda and I were laughing hysterically. Like years ago when we were little girls, sisters who were best friends. Sisters who shared a room, drank make-believe tea, and parented baby dolls. Tears of laughter rolled down her cheeks. I wanted to wipe them off, taste the salt of my first best friend, but I was laughing so hard.

We each strained to take a breath and then without hesitation, simultaneously words spilled out, "Remember Grandma's tablecloth?"

"You were pretty brave back then hiding the evidence," I said.

"I didn't hide it, you did. You wrinkled it up and threw it in the back of Megan and Laura's closet."

I knew it wasn't me, but thought better of arguing—as the youngest, I was always wrong. The truth is I was afraid to be questioned or judged. I was never sure what their reaction would be to my response, so I tried to control myself from laughing at the absurdity, my perfect sister. I wouldn't win. I couldn't win.

"Well, guess it doesn't matter now; we were both so worried."

"We were scared shitless. We had done the unthinkable. We had taken Grandma's cloth out of the drawer, the one Mama told us never to go into?"

"But it was so tempting, and we had that new tea set we had gotten for Christmas. Remember we wanted something really special for the first time we used it?"

"And then I filled the pitcher with grape juice and you moved your cup before I was finished, the grape juice spilled all over the tablecloth."

"And you screamed at me and didn't talk to me for a week, I was afraid you would never talk to me again." Sometimes, I wish she wouldn't. It was always the same. She talked to me, Megan and Laura did that too. They all talked to me, not with me, I felt so insignificant and worthless.

"I think it was New Year's. We had both forgotten, or almost anyway, and Mama couldn't find the cloth."

"We both started crying. Mama was so worried about us, comforting us."

"Making us cry harder."

"Then we took each other's hand and went together to get it out of Megan and Laura's closet. It was still in the corner, wadded up just like we had left it."

"Like you had left it."

"Mama took it from our hands. I'll never forget how sad she looked, how disappointed she seemed."

"I remember her laughing."

"Mama walked us both over to the sink and sat us up on top of the washing machine so we could watch."

"She was like a surgeon and a magician. She worked so carefully, putting the bleach in a cup and using that little brush."

"I always wanted to brush my teeth with it, I thought it would make them whiter." Together, we were there, at that moment years ago.
"And she scrubbed, not too hard, but just hard enough. We watched as the stain got lighter and lighter and pretty soon, swish it was gone."
"Mama still says swish sometimes, and I always remember that day."
"She put us back on the floor and prepared the washing machine."
"She looked so hurt. I don't ever think I've forgotten how disappointed she was," I said.
"I remember her laughing and smiling."
"And she said, 'Remember this and don't ever take things that aren't yours; you may not be so lucky next time.'" I thought about how true those words were. "We were so lucky, and no one can get cloths clean like Mama can. When she set the New Year's table that year, no one would have ever known what happened."

"Not even Grandma. And for that moment mama really didn't seem to care, did she?"

We both became silent and I found myself sitting on the floor, my hand in Miranda's lap. I couldn't believe we were holding hands. I felt the warmth and the frailty along with the roughness that had long ago replaced what had once been hands capable of modeling. I squeezed gently, not wanting to hurt her, but not wanting to let go. It had been so long. I think she pulled away, I'm not certain and perhaps it doesn't matter, because that second or two was enough to fill me, renew me.

Miranda sent me into the basement; even though she hadn't been down there for months, maybe years, she seemed to know exactly where everything was. A human GPS, she gave directions. "You'll find some packing boxes, folded up to the left of the stairs. They are behind the old radio, just behind it but not as far back as David's crib."

She was right on the money. There were stacks of boxes and each had been broken down, flattened, and stacked by size. I pulled out what I could carry in one trip and made my way back upstairs, where I was once again directed into the basement to find the packing tape and tape gun on the top shelf of the cabinet to the right of Peter's old workbench. As I put the boxes together, double-taping and securing the tape down with my nails to make sure it could not easily be removed, (a lesson we had all been taught by Papa—one of the few lessons each of us actually used) Miranda watched. I began putting each pile I had made into a designated box when Miranda stopped me. Instead, she directed me to unfold each item, examining it for true stains or spots. Anything designated spot or stain-free went in one box; those with stains or spots, which was almost everything, got divided among the four additional boxes. Miranda smiled slyly and satisfied at the finished job, not once thanking me, when she half-asked, half-told me she wanted me to go through Angela and David's baby things as well.

Once again, I was sent down into the basement. Directed to the bottom of the stairs, told to make a U-turn, walk back into the laundry room, turn left through the door. There I would find a wall of shelving. Midway down that wall on the second shelf from the left, I would find eight boxes, four marked Angela and four marked David. Obediently, I obliged, making eight separate trips, and waited for additional instructions. Miranda asked me to open the boxes and move them closer so she could help me as we went through them, again instructing me to make separate piles. Anything with a stain or spot went in one pile and those few items that were spotless or stainless went in another pile. I packed them accordingly, closed the boxes, and taped them, securing the tape with my nail (just as Papa had taught us.) When this was finished, we were both surprised how quickly the days had passed.

We had just enough time for dinner before it was time for bed as I had an early airplane to catch back home. I worried about what Miranda would do with the boxes; she had given me no instruction other than to pile them up in front of the closet, telling me she would take care of them. As I said good night and went upstairs to Angela's bedroom where I could change my clothes and relax after another long day of work, I couldn't help but wonder how she would do this. As she let me out of the car at the airport, I was sure it was just the stress of sitting at the curb too long—she forgot to tell me it was fun, forgot to say she enjoyed having me visit, forgot to say thanks. She pulled away before I even had time to turn around and wave goodbye. My job was done, until my next visit, when I would be needed and I would be back.

Months later, I was at Mama's when she was just finishing packing some boxes, Miranda's boxes. Miranda had sent Mama all the boxes I had packed for her and asked her to get the spots and stains out, to make them new again. Mama was so thrilled, so honored. I hadn't seen Mama glow like that for a very long time. As Mama packed the last box, I helped her tape it shut. I secured the tape with my nail (just as Papa had taught us). Mama put her hand on mine and smiled at me. She looked so peaceful and proud, so full of love when she asked me if she could wash Kristy, Grace, and Matthew's baby clothes too. Of course, I told her, I'd gladly pull them out and bring them by. When I got home and pulled out the boxes. I began to go through them, each onesie, each sweater, overalls, bibs—every stain, each spot brought back a memory. Kristy's first taste of peas, the grape jelly that always found itself more on Grace's fingers than in her mouth, Matthew's spit up. Grass stains from crawling in the backyard, sand stains from that first trip to the beach, blood stains from a bloody nose. Memories that no matter how much I wanted to add to Mama's smile, they were memories I couldn't bear to let her erase by washing them away.

I went back to Mama's empty-handed and told her how I felt. Mama took my hand and in silence, we walked through the house up to her bedroom where, from her closet, she took out a small box. We sat down together on her bed where she opened the box, inside neatly folded were four infant layettes, one that belonged to each of her four daughters, each still had a small stain.

a light (in a darkened corner)
two small fragments of the sun
light, speedily growing brighter
bringing together all the joy and happiness it can find.

Remaining death sober
I fear not the empty house
which I must now enter
or the painful loneliness
which strikes my every now and then
I neither fear
the stillness of waiting
just afraid of being nowhere at all
without myself

morning has just broken into my hour
my room of sleep it has not been rude
but instead polite it has knocked on my window
and asked me to
open my shade
everything is beginning to melt under the suns bright light
and
soon
spring will be here
it feels like spring today, everything looks so alive and smells
so fresh
the birds singing so cheerfully, the trees stretching upward
from their long winter sleep
everything is waking up
even people
I saw so many smiles
I can only hope they are saying thank you to the sun for
another beautiful day

GIRLS' NIGHT

Girls' Night

Between them, they had eleven children, three grandchildren, five dogs, two cats, a bird and had been married one hundred thirty-eight years.

They had promised to "love, honor, and cherish, for better or for worse, for richer, for poorer, in sickness and in health," and now they were stuck. Each of them for their own reason, but all of them feeling unable to walk away, honoring the commitment "until death do us part."

How many times had each of them silently prayed "until death do us part" like an old LP with a scratch, playing over and over again, until someone would get up and move the needle? But like so many baby boomers whose lives had become stale and stuck, there was no simple fix. Moving the needle only meant holding their breaths, waiting for that next scratch, until that was all that was left. One big scratch.

In the early years, when they had young children and/or careers, they were too busy to notice the flaws. Perhaps they noticed but cared enough about their pledges to let it go. Perhaps it was their children, their jobs, their lives moving along in a forward motion the way they had been taught or learned as children themselves that allowed them to stay. But now with empty houses, retired from jobs, home alone with the partner they never really knew, they were time bombs and their houses battlefields, no one knowing who or when the next explosion would go off. It wasn't hard for the women to realize that they had indeed been one another's salvation over the years. They celebrated birthdays, new jobs, promotions, weight loss and, in the later years, graduations, weddings, grandchildren.

Over the years, they had also learned to mourn together: the death of a sibling, a parent, the aging process, cancer. They had been there for each other, to celebrate each other. But in reality, none of them were prepared for the desperation they felt in their marriages and the camaraderie alone proved not to be enough.

It hit Claire the hardest when her youngest moved across the country to live in California; her oldest had taken a job in Vegas a few years earlier. His move had hit her hard, but with her daughter home, it was tolerable. Now she was lost. She wasn't sure that the house was big enough with just the two of them. It had been seven years since her retirement as an event planner; she had retired just before Katie had gone away to school, hoping they'd have some special mother-daughter time. They had, and for that, she was grateful, but after Katie left for school, it wasn't as wonderful as she'd hoped. She had a hard time getting motivated. Nick was distant, or maybe she was; either way, it wasn't what she'd expected. She had always been the one who could plan the perfect celebration and used her small stature to her advantage. Claire had learned through the years that her small size meant big charm, and rarely could anyone turn down that little woman with big blue eyes that screamed, "Don't you dare say no or I'll roll over and die." It was the sheer guilt of saying no that got her just what she always wanted, and usually that turned out to be a win-win for the vendor/venue and the client and, of course, always for Claire. Back in the day, she was known in her field as the powerhouse. She could always get the best deal and make even the lowest-budget event look like they'd spent a million.

Now, the husbands of her very best friends referred to that powerhouse as the instigator. The same men who had asked for her help and advice now blamed her for their own unhappy relationships. The times that the couples would get together had become uncomfortable. Claire spent hours trying to remember conversations, trying to remember if any of them had ever voiced their unhappiness or, like her, did they just ignore it, hold it in, pretend that "happily ever after" existed in their homes? Now when they got together and she'd listen, hear their unhappiness, hear their frustrations, hear the "until death do us part," her wheels began spinning and she began to think of ways she could help. Because, echoing in her head were those very same words, "until death do us part." What seemed hopeless became hopeful when the women discovered a local comedy club and found themselves as more than frequent attendees.

The first time they went to the comedy club was more a cry for help than just a good night to go out. Michelle and Claire had been friends since grammar school. They were friends who even when absence, distance, business, or family prevented them from talking were able to pick up from wherever they had left off.

Michelle had called Claire late in the day, crying. Her husband, Rob, the high-powered engineer, wanted her to have another plastic surgery. He thought her boobs sagged and didn't like how old that made her look, or the reality of how old it made him feel. She had realized after the last plastic surgery, a tummy tuck—that enough was enough. The sacrifices she made for his pleasure, for his success; she was tired of it all. She dreamed of going back to school, of taking the LSAT, and making law school a reality, no longer satisfied with the liberal arts degree she had received so that Rob would never feel threatened by her career. He had earned his engineering degree, graduating top of his class and yet, even after thirty years, she still wasn't quite certain what his job entailed.

She told Claire it wasn't just a drink she needed; she needed a good laugh. Claire listened as Michelle continued to vent. She and Rob hardly talked anymore and dinner together meant watching TV, not even anything good. He didn't even seem to care about the kids or grandkids. "... and really why would I want to get a boob lift? I've been sleeping in Alison's room for months. If I so much as touched him in bed, he'd grunt that angry Rob grunt. I'm not even sure what sex is," Michelle half-laughed.

Claire comforted her, promising the perfect night out and got busy gathering the troops. She was surprised when almost everyone was not only available, but also raring to get out. They agreed to meet in the parking lot at six forty-five, a good hour plus before the doors opened. The only one not sure if she could make it was Jillian and Claire was secretly pleased even though Jillian, who of course hated being left out of anything, promised to try to join in later. Claire assured her it wasn't necessary, that there would be plenty of other times.

Claire was happy that the container of slush she had in the freezer hadn't been touched and whipped up some grilled veggies and goat cheese, along with a bag of blue corn chips to bring along. She had always hated having a minivan, but thought how on occasions like this, it definitely came in handy. Her own traveling party wagon.

She picked up Stephanie at five thirty, hoping they'd have a little time alone. Stephanie was the youngest of the women and always caught Claire up on all the latest trends. Stephanie had a one-car family and when Anthony heard she was going out, he was quick to make plans with his ex and their son. He'd be using the car. Claire smiled to herself as Stephanie came out, camera over her shoulder. Claire couldn't remember ever seeing Stephanie without her camera; she loved to document everything. Claire knew it was wrong, but took a sip of slush from the travel coffee mug, and then handed another full mug to Stephanie, whose response as she took a drink was "You are a terrible influence... you know that? Right?" Claire waved at Anthony who pulled out in front of her.

"He's in a hurry, huh?" Stephanie explained his evening plans as she took another big sip from her mug.

Stephanie's was a late-life marriage. In her early forties, she thought she had waited for a reason, finally finding true love in Anthony. But it wasn't long after the wedding that the honeymoon wore off. Stephanie, who had a successful career of her own, was finding it difficult to share life with Anthony, much less his ten-year-old son, Tony. And while Tony didn't live with them, there was way more contact and communication between Anthony and his ex than Stephanie was comfortable with. And then there were the constant comparisons that came up when they got together with Anthony and his ex's old friends. She was so grateful for having met Claire and the other women and being included, a new friendship that was hers and on the occasion that the couples got together, theirs.

By the time Sarah and Michelle had arrived in the parking lot, Stephanie and Claire had already had a few refills each. Stephanie had been busy snapping photos as she and Claire were giggling, making faces not only at each other but anyone who might pass by and glance their way. This included the unusually tall, bird-like woman who really had them going as she stood there for a bit, making faces back, and then kindly excused herself as Sarah and Michelle walked around her to get in the van. Michelle was quick to grab her drink and some of the chips and veggies that Claire had forgotten to open for her and Stephanie. Sarah scooped out slush too, but hesitated with the chips. Sarah was always watching her weight, often letting her being overweight get in the way of allowing herself to succeed. Although her friends weren't sure if it was her weight or her husband Brian that was the cause of her insecurity. Brian had been out of work for eight years, and it was a bit of an embarrassment to Sarah.

Brian stayed at home, but was definitely not a stay-at-home dad. Brian who had at one time been the apple of Sarah's eye was now just a festering sore. She drove more than an hour a day, just so she could work eight hours to go home to a house full of dishes, dirty laundry, and a hungry family, including Brian. Her daughters did not meet her expectations and she spent hours helping them with homework only so that they would get C's. She bought DVD's that taught beauty techniques and, as the girls grew up, asked her friends to have their children include hers. Her pain was two-fold and she was lost in a way that the others tried to understand. It wasn't just Brian's lack of productivity and attentiveness, his pure laziness and failed success that hurt, but the imperfections she saw in her own daughters that at times left her overwhelmed. It was this pain that her friends liked to see wash away with a good laugh and the camaraderie of their friendship, often easier said than done.

After the first drink went down a little quicker than anticipated, Sarah explained that it had been an exceptionally long day. Her words flowed. "So I got another call from the bank today. Brian's been shopping a bit too much and the auto-pay funds for the mortgage were insufficient. When I asked him about it, he denied any such expenses. Of course I didn't believe him; after all, the bank called. INSUFFICIENT FUNDS!!!! Really," Sarah let Stephanie fill her mug again. "So I pushed and do you know what that SOB told me? He said it was a surprise for me and now I'd ruined it..." Sarah took a large sip. "He hung up on me!" She took another gulp and watched out the window, waiting for something, or as it turned out, someone. Claire responded that Jillian would be quite late, if she made it at all, which allowed Sarah to indulge herself a bit more than usual. She hated how as close as she and Jillian were, she always had to worry about being judged. Even as schoolgirls, Jillian would always be judging. "Don't eat that, it'll make you fat. You really should cut your hair at the beauty salon instead of letting your mom do it." She was especially judgmental of Sarah's "imperfect" daughters and pushed Sarah to interfere with their day-to-day activities until she didn't know how not to. As an adult, Sarah wondered how Jillian had the nerve to judge anyone else when she was constantly behaving inappropriately and without concern of others so that she could get ahead. Sometimes she even questioned how they were even friends.

Michelle, who had had a drink or two earlier in the day, didn't need too much encouragement to begin the husband bashing, and as each woman comfortably allowed herself, they chimed in. The van rocked with allegations of neglect and laziness, always concluding with "that fucking asshole."

By the time they made it into the comedy club, the first act had just finished up and they were grateful that they could be seated so quickly. Claire noticed the face-making woman serving drinks and quickly made a dash towards her, only to be held back by the sheer crowd of full tables. The woman looked up from the table she was serving when she saw the commotion out of the corner of her eye and recognized them as well. She made a face, causing uproarious laughter from Claire and Stephanie, and motioned them to a table in her section. The first thing Claire did when they sat down and the woman came over was to give her a big hug. Claire was a hugger and like it or not, if one was in her space and the mood presented itself, one would be smack dab in a full-blown hug.

Dodie introduced herself before asking if they were ready to order. Stephanie, who was normally most able to remain somewhat professional in any situation, started to giggle. Dodie actually looked a bit like a dodo bird, her thick glasses magnified her closely set small eyes and her ears stuck out just a bit through her mousy brown hair. Her thin nose was a bit bigger than most and had just the slightest curve down, almost like a beak. But there was also something quite beautiful about her, perhaps her smile, with her straight white teeth, or the way she held herself despite her unusual size for a woman, or maybe even a man. She had a confidence about her that almost made Stephanie envious.

Despite the fact that they drank more than their share in the van, they ordered a pitcher of margaritas. They ate and drank and laughed. Dodie came back with the check at the thirty-minute warning, last call. Just fifteen minutes before the end of the show, Jillian came rushing through the door, causing not just a commotion but a slew of lewd remarks from the comedian as well as boos from the audience. Jillian jumped right in, as if she owned the table, grabbing the pitcher and filling Sarah's half-empty glass with the last drop and then picked it up and finished it. No one said anything. Jillian immediately began complaining about how her husband, Mitchel, had become so apathetic with her that he didn't even care about their lack of intimacy lately. She didn't apologize for her tardiness but rather gloatingly began to explain.

"You know George was staying late tonight, I just figured it'd be the perfect opportunity to give him something extra when he starts making decisions for the upcoming promotion." No one wanted to hear it at this point, causing the entire table's vibe to change. Dodie never came back, and it was the last time that Jillian missed a girls' night out.

The comedy venue was the perfect escape and before long, the women found themselves going twice a month, if not more. It wasn't long before Mitchel began organizing husbands for guys' nights out as well. When the women heard, they joked about Mitchel taking on such a role. Mitchel was quiet, not quite as quiet and non-descript as Nick, Claire's husband, but quiet in a Ted Bundy sort of way. From their early years, Mitchel had watched Jillian push and shove her way to the top. He never said too much, even when it was he being pushed. The women noticed, often feeling almost sorry for him, and wondering why he continued to work with her, instead of finding a job somewhere else, especially when Jillian would gloat about how she had painfully humiliated him in front of upper management just to assure that he wouldn't be the one to get the next promotion. Jillian always demanded being in charge of everything and everyone, letting Mitchel get ahead or one up on her might jeopardize all of that. She always had the need to be the best—or at least appear that way; perfection was everything to her. If Mitchel got the promotion, Jillian was afraid what people might think about her inability to be the best. He always remained quiet. Mitchel had spent years in her shadows, silently watching her cheat and sometimes steal. He didn't so much mind working all day and then going home to take care of the kids when they were young, and found pride in contributing to their positive attitudes and high self-esteem. But now that the kids were grown and gone, he still worked all day, but going home to complete the household chores wasn't fun and the satisfaction he may have felt in cooking and cleaning were stamped out by the degrading comments Jillian made when she came home. Doing anything that made him feel good was sure not to satisfy Jillian, and of late, his sexual performance, which had satisfied her all these years, wasn't good enough. Something had to change and over drinks one night at the bowling alley with the other husbands he knew just what it was.

. . . .

Mitchel was pleased when everyone had agreed to join him, even Nick, who always preferred being alone rather than bother with small talk or commitment. But on nights when they got together, he actually enjoyed listening to the guys complain about their significant others and surprised even himself how comfortable he was chiming in. "She never shuts up." In recent years since the kids had left, he was increasingly irritated with Claire's excessive ranting. He hated that he couldn't make a move without thinking she was judging, that she only cooked foods she liked, that her music made him nauseous, that the house smelled from incense, and that the television was always on Oxygen or Lifetime.

Brian added a dimension to the group that no one else could; after all he had no ethics and no responsibilities. He was the one guaranteed to bring a laugh to the worst of nights, and as the good-looking comedian had no trouble attracting the younger women if they so desired to play. Brian had never really wanted kids, much less to have a job that would tie him to one house, one town, one anything for very long. He planned on after marrying Sarah, they would travel, follow whatever band was cool at the time, smoke dope and drink tequila, and party hardy. He figured odd jobs would be enough to get them by and that they would both be romantically satisfied; that they would live on the very richness of their love. Sarah got pregnant on their honeymoon, and Madison was born ten months after Michaela.

Brian's experience with a nine to five job was less than positive and his ability to parent not much better. Going out with the guys and an opportunity to wife bash was just what Brian needed.

No one really liked Rob, but he too brought something to the table. Rob liked being the big spender with his friends and showing off that he could afford almost anything. And with his arrogance waning, he was a bit more tolerable. Recently, he had begun touching up his black hair, hiding any gray, and he began to wear sweaters to cover up his midsection flab. The guys found it amusing, but Rob, whose parents had recently died, began to sense his own mortality. He was too young to give in. He needed something, someone different, someone young with life and drive and sex. He had had enough. He was so glad to be included.

Mitchel, Nick, Brian, and Rob had history, although they seldom communicated independently of the time they spent as couples socializing; they had watched one another's families grow up, watched one another's marriages become distant and although they were silent in their memories or willingness to verbalize, they were somewhat pleased and relieved that they had this connection.

The inclusion of Stephanie's husband Anthony was an after-thought, but Mitchel invited him, afraid that leaving him out would seem socially unacceptable and Jillian would never expect him to do anything that wasn't appropriate or socially correct.

After several months of coordinating nights out, Mitchel showed up to the bar with Duane, a work friend. Mitchel had met Duane at the Chemco office. Mitchel had gone in early one morning and Duane, the fourth floor maintenance man, was just finishing up. They struck up a friendly conversation, which turned into an hour-long discussion on exploring the molecular genetics and biochemical changes in germplasm and the political climate of Chemco. Mitchel was surprised to hear Jillian's name come up and let it slide, not wanting to make it personal. Mitchel liked Duane, but was curious how he ended up doing maintenance. Not wanting to appear too nosey he used his security clearance, which allowed him access to employee records.

Duane held a Ph.D. in chemistry, although he hadn't worked in the field. Right after graduation, there was a family tragedy. His parents had fought for years and after one such occasion, his mom had one drink too many. She took the car and left; an hour later, she drove into a local reservoir and died. Duane blamed his father and no longer could remain calm and collected, as his mom had always requested. He beat his father with a baseball bat until he was unconscious and then sat down and waited for the police to arrive. He spent the next five years in the county jail and only got out because of overcrowding and good behavior. He had no relationship with his father, never wanting to see him again and he could not care less that his father spent his days being cared for in a state nursing home. He blamed his father for his career being over before it had even begun, and he felt grateful when a maintenance position opened up at Chemco, a company known for hiring ex-felons as part of the federal tax credit program. He hoped that someday it would open other doors. With a background like that, Mitchel's wheels turned and he was anxious to bring Duane into his circle and have everyone meet him.

Everyone liked Duane. He was an easy to like guy and fun to be around; no one seemed to mind when he joined them. The next step was somehow introducing Duane to all of their wives. Duane already knew who Jillian was, and Mitchel was pretty confident she wouldn't recognize him; he was far too unimportant for her. He invited Duane and his girlfriend to their annual pre-Thanksgiving open house.

....

After that first late arrival, Jillian was never late again, often coming early so they wouldn't have to sit in Dodie's station. She didn't like her, nothing about her—her looks, how confident she was, how she wasn't bothered by Jillian's antagonizing words or stares. She especially didn't like the fraternizing between her and her friends. But without fail, Claire, Stephanie, Michelle, and even Sarah would somehow change tables and end up with Dodie. Growing up ignored by peers, Dodie had learned an amazing talent, to listen. Some people called it eavesdropping; Dodie liked to think of it as learning. In this case, she hoped perhaps a way to help. As was most often the case, the women came in drunk or buzzed, but readily accepted the pitcher of margaritas—their signature drink— and then immediately, the husband bashing began.

Dodie noticed Claire's stance change, her posture became more assertive and when she leaned in, Dodie was very careful to learn. Claire started. "Enough... haven't we all had enough? We come here week after week, month after month, and each time, we have to go home, back to the same people that we come here to escape. Has anyone seen 'Horrible Bosses'?" Stephanie laughed; she had seen it. In fact, Anthony and she had watched it together and loved it. "Well, I want everyone to watch it, because my dears, we are going to remake it for real; we are going to remake it as, Horrible Husbands." She put her hand up with a fist full of straws extending out, each straw had a name. "This is your horrible husband. Don't tell anyone who you get and after you watch the movie, you'll understand." Sarah chose a straw, but wasn't willing to wait to watch the movie to understand.

"Just a hint, Claire, what's it about?" Stephanie smiled. Claire hesitated and then gave a brief explanation.

"It's about a group of friends who all work for deplorable bosses and decide to get revenge by killing them. Not their own, that would be too obvious. So they agree to get rid of each other's. Get it? Horrible Husbands." Sarah smiled. She poured herself another margarita and chugged it. Stephanie gave her one of those "really" looks, and Claire actually responded with, "Yep." Stephanie just shook her head as each woman cautiously and with great seriousness, pulled a straw. Stephanie took what was left, not sure she really wanted to be included; at least she'd have to see how to get Anthony removed. Dodie so wanted to chime in; it had been one of her favorite movies. She and her boyfriend had watched it, discussing how easy it would have been to actually pull off. Instead, she came to the table, asking if they were ready for refills.

. . . .

Mitchel approached Duane with kid gloves, more as a hypothetical question than a proposition. While it was Mitchel who had the idea of getting rid of the women, it was Duane who actually came up with the final plan. Mitchel explained the details, assuring them that no one would have to get their hands dirty. This was the perfect solution, a business deal that allowed each of them to be once removed. To put it simply, each of them would pay in seventy-five hundred dollars and provide access information and places their wives frequented; schedules should be included. In exchange, they would not be told when or where and they were never to ask questions or know who it was that was carrying out the acts. They would never reveal their intent or discuss the arrangements to anyone outside of the six of them. They were not to push the issue with Mitchel and were not to ever question the source. It would be up to each of them to secure their own innocence.

It was a doable amount, even for Brian, and within days, everyone had paid in. Anthony had been the odd man out in the beginning, after all he was Claire's friend first, but even if he wasn't sure, it was too late and he too was in, at least for now.

. . . .

The comedy club was loud and the women, who were trying to be a bit more discreet than usual, found themselves yelling to be heard. Jillian was first. "I loved it. Claire, you're brilliant... Horrible Bosses/Horrible Husbands. You are a genius!" Dodie leaned in over Jillian's shoulder to put down the glasses. Jillian thought she looked a little too interested and turned quickly, pushing her a bit. "Excuse me, do you mind?" Dodie continued to put the glasses around the table before leaving. She was getting sick of Jillian's treatment and didn't understand how everyone else put up with her. Her own wheels began to turn.

Jillian wanted to talk plans and ideas but was quickly shut up as the plan was to be discreet and not shared with the world. The only consensus was when to begin and the answer was immediately after the holidays, New Year's included. Again, Claire stressed, "No one should know anything, and I mean anything. Also, there is to be no obvious brutality and each act has to be quick and appear to be an accident. It is up to each of you to secure your own innocence."

. . . .

Mitchel answered the door, while Jillian looked pretty and mingled. Duane introduced Mitchel to the unusually tall, bird-like woman who held onto his arm. "This is my girlfriend, Dodie," Duane proudly continued, "and Dodie, this is Mitchel." Dodie was as surprised to see Claire and Sarah as they were to see her. Suddenly, the playing field had changed, when she realized that these were the women Duane had told her about. Most of them women she liked and considered friends. Claire and Sarah saw Dodie come in and quickly tried to play interception, knowing how Jillian felt about her. They liked her and wanted to protect her. But Jillian, who had already had one too many, couldn't be stopped.

"What are you doing in my house?" She grabbed for Dodie's arm. Duane caught her first and one thing led to another with Duane and Dodie making apologies to Mitchel to leave. Mitchel, embarrassed by his wife's behavior, attempted to apologize as well.

. . . .

Dodie had told Duane about the women she had so wanted to be friends with, describing each one in detail. How ironic that it was these people, with their "perfect" lives, nice cars and houses who had committed to the ultimate betrayal. Now they realized that both the women and men that had been plotting to do away with their spouses were indeed the husbands and wives they knew, respectfully. It wasn't hard for Duane and Dodie to come up with a plan of their own. The question wasn't if, but when.

. . . .

The next week when they met at the comedy club, it was awkward. Everyone wanted Jillian to apologize, but she wouldn't hear of it. Dodie, who had a new girl with her when she came to the table, attempted to act as if it hadn't happened. But Stephanie could see that she was troubled. Dodie introduced Melissa, a bubbly young college girl, explaining that she was going away for a while. She said she thought they'd like Melissa, so she would be taking over her tables, "especially my favorites," she emphasized. They hadn't expected such a quick goodbye and were all visibly saddened at her announcement. At the end of the night, Claire gave Dodie a big hug, so did Stephanie, Michelle and Sarah, all of them wanting to know when she'd be back. They left her a huge tip with all of their contact information, everyone but Jillian.

．．．．．．．．．．．．．．．．．

It was a cold morning in January when the women arrived at the funeral home, each with their husbands uncomfortably at their sides. The casket was open and Mitchel had that look of submission that Jillian so liked. Claire wondered how the mortician had accomplished that. The funeral home was full; in fact, they had to open up the sliding walls and use two rooms. To look around, you would think Mitchel was the best of the best. The women and their husbands got in line to pay their respects. Mitchel and Jillian's adult children sitting in the front row; overcome with sorrow, Jillian stood in front of the casket, trying to be emotional but instead acting the perfect hostess. After the line had cleared and the husbands had been seated, the women joined Jillian for one last time in front of the casket; they joined hands and squeezed. They were silent, not sure as they glanced at one another if they should laugh or cry.

Independently, each feared for the other with unknown and uncertain feelings. They sat with Jillian, offering their support throughout the service. They listened as Rob gave a eulogy, but all of them were anxious to leave. It was when they were walking out that Stephanie noticed Duane in the back row just getting up to leave. He was with a beautiful tall woman whose obvious taste in clothes sang model and for a moment, Stephanie felt a slight pang of sadness for Dodie's loss, but then the woman lifted her dark sunglasses and their eyes met. Stephanie could see that same confidence, that beautiful smile, and a cold chill came over her as the woman nodded and, putting her glasses back on, walked away.

I sat silent, listening to her telling me her life
while on my lap I held her youngest child
and I watched her as her nose ran and she
caught it in her mouth
Her hands were worn yet she sported jewels
that she bragged were worth thousands
the mink coat that draped her shoulders was
better cared for and cleaner then this small
child I held upon my lap
nose running, knotted hair
She spoke with eyes a glimmer of many
marriages pointing to the children that
surrounded me each child a trophy of another
marriage and as she spoke I realized how
lonely she really was

Slowly dying away are my patience
of hope
and my anxiety of helpless hours
where I laid alone at night,
(they are finally disappearing into
darkness)
as I sat alone last evening peering
into my past
I stopped at a familiar face and tried
reaching out
for it
but just like now as soon and
quickly as it came it was gone.
everything is gone, so alone
I try and reach
myself

SAYING GOODBYE

Saying Goodbye

I wonder who you complain to, or to whom you file a report, when for four days in a row the weathermen are wrong. "Perfect day again, as we have clear skies and more sunshine." Really, where are they looking? Certainly not here outside my house? No, there is certainly no sun shining here. It is dull and gloomy, so uninviting that I don't even want to leave home. Forcing myself just to go to the grocery store when I realize we've run out of creamer. I wouldn't bother, but the lack of sun most definitely requires caffeine, and I haven't yet learned the art of drinking my coffee black.

I feel anxious driving, waiting for a thunderstorm to start, worrying about finding a parking space, wondering what I'll do if they are out of Fat Free Original. Once, just after the company had decided to change their label design, I mistakenly picked up a bottle of Low Fat Vanilla. I'm sure it had been wrongfully placed in the Fat Free Original spot. I didn't want to be wasteful or be stuck drinking my coffee with skim milk or worse yet, whipping cream, so I was stuck and it ruined two weeks of my morning coffee.

Today, what I notice as I sit down with my third cup of the day is that the gloom has snuck into my house as well. Tired, I close my eyes, and listen. It is so quiet that I can hear the humming of the refrigerator, the ticking of the battery-powered clock in the den, and I'm quite certain I can even hear the sound of my own pulse. It is an unsettling quiet, a reminder of the loneliness that has engulfed my world and our house. It is a loneliness that I thought I had overcome, perhaps even risen above, but now I'm not sure. When I was working full time, I talked to Carl once or twice during the day, but not anymore. No, he has made it quite clear that he is too busy to be talking to me on the phone all day and so when he leaves for work until he gets home, we don't speak. Lately, we don't have much to say to each other even then. I have become a shell, and an empty one at that.

It is difficult not to let my mind wander as I reminisce about all those years that I worked at A Place Called Hope, a social service organization dedicated to keeping at-risk families together. All the time that I joyfully gave of myself to helping others, I realize now it somehow had made me feel complete. Useful. Needed. Every family, each child, the stories that they shared and the incidents they remembered. There wasn't a family I didn't remember, a child I didn't know, or a name I could forget. Working at the Hope had given me substance.

I think about my children, how patient they were, sharing so many Mommy hours with complete strangers. I think about how compassionate they have become. I think about them and remember.

Whenever we were together, which I see now was never enough, there was their laughter; there was their arguing, their lengthy discussions and most of all, there was their loving. I wrap my arms around myself, trying to recreate one of their many hugs. To feel their warmth and one-time neediness wrapped around me. To feel both their pleasures, their insecurities and their pride. I miss them. When they were home and growing up, there was so much to talk about. There was their homework and the variety of school functions. There were sporting events and band practice, dating and adolescent uncertainty. With the children home, Carl and I always had something to share, to talk about. And if it wasn't the children, we would sometimes just talk about work, both Carl's job and mine. But that was then.

What was I thinking when I decided to leave Hope, welcoming a younger me to take over? She was so enthusiastic and vibrant, the stories not yet branded into her soul. All the time in the world to embrace, reach out, help. I hadn't really thought it through. I hadn't realized that my children didn't need me anymore, not the same way they needed me when they were small and I didn't realize how soon after I left that they both had plans that meant they were not only moving out, but moving on. That Kristin would be getting married, and that their plans didn't include moving next door. I didn't realize that Carl would be reaching his own midlife turmoil, with little room or compassion for mine.

As I continue to drink my third cup of coffee, which is now cold, I wonder. What now? For days now, tears seem to drip indiscriminately down my cheeks and I find myself doing nothing, more than I do something. I think about my aging parents. Mom, why didn't you ever tell me how empty I would feel? Was it easier for you back then? Was it because there were so many of us that you and Dad couldn't wait to be alone? I can't be alone.

I think about my best friend, Karen. When she called last year and asked me to meet her at the hospital, I didn't really think about why; her voice screamed that it was urgent. I dropped everything to be with her. It was late and I remember it had been raining for days. The temperature had dropped to freezing and the roads were sheets of ice. Just walking from the parking lot into the emergency room, I was soaked, cold, and shaking. I was almost as petrified of hospitals as I was of death. I wasn't prepared. The first thing I saw was Rebecca, Karen's younger daughter, her head buried in her parents' chests—their arms wrapped around her. It was obvious that even they weren't capable of giving what comfort was needed. But when Karen saw me standing there, it was she who made the first move. She had been crying—that was obvious—but there was also an awkward calm about her. She put her arms around me, concerned for my comfort, and then quietly whispered.

"Alice, she's gone. My Margo's gone. It was fast; I thank God it was fast. She's at peace now. Jesus held his arms open and she ran to him. Oh, Alice, Margo went home." I'll never forget her words. I remember because I didn't know if I wanted to run away, be sick, or was just envious of her faith. Karen, my dear friend, was a devout Christian and she truly believed Margo, her eldest daughter, was in a better place. I wanted to shake her, I wanted to scream, that there was no better place than here. Right here with her mom, dad, and little sister who idolized her. Right here with family and friends. Right here going to school dances, college, getting married, and someday having a family of her own, making Karen a grandma. I wanted to scream, but Karen was so sure, so certain, so at peace.

I hate death. Just the idea of it scares me. How can we be left so alone? What happens? It was then, there at the hospital on the evening of Margo's death that I first thought about the options. It was there that I knew I didn't want to ever be the one left behind, to be the one missing, the one left to mourn. No, I would have to go first. Shortly after the funeral or as Karen called it, the celebration, the sending off, I got a call from Oliver, my friend Kate's husband. Through the sobs, I could barely make out the words "Kate is gone, Alice. Her parents found her, no note, no warning, she just left." Unlike Karen, Oliver's faith wavered. Oliver had two young children at home. "What am I going to tell them, Alice? What the fuck did she do?" He was so angry. I had just talked to Kate and she had mentioned that they had lost some of the romance. She wondered if she really wanted to make it work; she talked about taking time off. I had no idea. "She talks to you; I know she does. What did she tell you?" he screamed with way too much blame.

No, I can't be left behind. But I can't leave like you did, Kate. As I think about it now, remembering like it was yesterday, I realize I have a purpose. I have to make every last day together, with those I love most, meaningful. I have to make the last memories of me the very best. Unlike Kate or Margo who just left, I will make certain to say goodbye. I will spend the next few days, maybe weeks if I have to—making plans, giving gifts. I finished my coffee and began. I took my cup to the sink to wash and realized I hadn't done the dishes for days. Not breakfast, lunch, or dinner dishes. I wonder didn't Carl notice. Did he say anything? I needed to clean up. I needed to make a list, maybe several. I would compartmentalize, divide the lists up by people and projects. Favorite activities, favorite foods, maybe things I hated but they loved. I know who the people are and there aren't many—Jason, Kristin, Carl, Mom, Dad. I think I'll list Karen separate from my other girlfriends. Yes, I'll have a list just for her. I don't want to include any of my brothers or sisters, certainly not aunts, uncles, or cousins. Time is precious and so are memories, but with so few memories already, what is the point in making new ones, just to say goodbye to those who don't even say hello. And so I start. I make a list of favorite foods, things I can freeze, things that I don't make often, splurges. I start by cleaning out the freezer and the refrigerator; I make my grocery list. I try to make a plan of what days I will make chicken potpies, lasagna, oyster stew, cheesecake, stuffed brownies, banana cream pie, blueberry scones. I decide to grate lots of cheese and freeze it with instructions for fondue—a family Christmas tradition. As a Jew by birth, and Carl born and raised a Protestant, neither of us had really found our way religiously. I mostly describe myself as an agnostic in progress. I decide my last plans will be with Karen. If there is a heaven, maybe her faith will send me safely on my way.

The list is easier than I thought. With purpose, I get up early each day and actually begin to look forward to its execution. I find that my family is more than accommodating when I begin inviting each of them to enjoy our day. My first date is with Justin, my eldest child. Justin surprises me by coming home the night before so that we can get an early start. We are awake before sunrise; I am grateful for the perfect weather. Justin and I hike to his favorite fishing spot. We find ourselves lucky, catching more than our fair share of bass and trout. We take home the morning's catch and I make a fish fry, leaving us plenty of time for a day of activities.

We go to the art institute and he spends hours sharing with me his interpretation of his favorite artists and their paintings. We grab a midday glass of wine at the corner café and are still finished early enough to get in a night Cubs game; amazingly the Cubs won.

It was a bit more difficult to work out the plans with Kristin. Doug, my son-in-law, didn't mind one night but Kristin wanted to make certain that it was the right timing. She comes by in the morning and we drive together to the spa. She talks nonstop, so excited to have this time together. We get all of her favorite treatments; we even get new color and hairstyles. She still enjoys this activity with me as much as I remember she always has. We enjoy the spa lunch and afterwards go to the video store where Kristin picks out her favorite movie, even though we've both seen it often enough to recite the lines along with the actors. We have ice cream and stuffed brownies for dinner and hot buttered popcorn in bed. We stay up late—more like friends than mother and daughter—and share secrets.

When I invited Mom, she was excited. She came over right after she made sure Dad had breakfast and a sandwich ready for lunch. We spend the morning cleaning out a closet I've left just for her. We watch the Food Channel and spend the rest of the day making a menu of choice. Dad meets her at our house, where the four of us enjoy our day's lesson. Which with Mom's perfection turns out just that, perfect. I make her blueberry scones that she argues about taking home for breakfast. She keeps saying, "You shouldn't have," and in the end, she thanks me and tells me how much she'll enjoy them in the morning.

I talk Dad into taking the day off and although he hates doing anything without Mom, the love of his life, I've convinced him and we watch his favorite western. We eat popcorn and he lies on the couch. We talk business and he explains to me for the hundredth time how to watch the stock market. We go through hundreds of his pictures on the computer and I'm interested; he has my undivided attention and I his.

The easiest plans are with my girlfriends, who are always up for a night out. We meet at my house first for drinks; we laugh until we cry. We go to the comedy club. We remember how lucky we are to have each other and how important these times are. They have become my lifeline over the last several years and I learn I have become theirs.

Making special plans with Carl, my sweet Carl, should have been easy, but working around his schedule was more difficult than I imagined. It took a while to find the perfect weekend. The weekend I chose, wanting to bring you forever happiness. We go for a long drive to nowhere. I watch one of your horror movies with you, we go to that brewery you've wanted to go to and I drink beer. I think you might faint when I don't throw up. I take Karen's advice and put a glass of hot water next to the bed. I surprise you by holding it to my mouth and after I spit it out, I put you in my mouth. You know how much I hate doing that, but you are in ecstasy. We hold each other all night, and we are both sad when the weekend ends and you have to go back to work.

Karen, we spend the day shopping, doing lunch, talking husbands and sharing secrets. We talk about Margo. We do what we always do; we love each other. Karen, I don't ever want you to feel guilty. You have always been my rock, my hope. It is you who makes me believe in peace.

I find myself sad when I find my list complete. It is a beautiful purpose making memories and I am so glad that I have chosen this path to say goodbye; perhaps I think I might just want to make a few more.

The phone rings. Alice has just gotten out of the shower; she hears the caller ID voice. "You have a call from Carl." As she rushes to answer it, she slips.

He leaves her a message, "Had a minute, just called to say I love you."

The autopsy results say she died instantly.

The flower
opening,
then,
growing,
reaching
with
everything
to
make it
to it's
"source"
(sun takes it's turn of
darkness)
growing
still stronger
the flower
leans upward
and you
hear it
whisper
"Help..."

lightened by darkness
which clouds my body
laughter tears apart
at my mind
as I dive through clouds
of
mirrored mazes
and come to a halt as the
westward fisherman
reels in the sun.

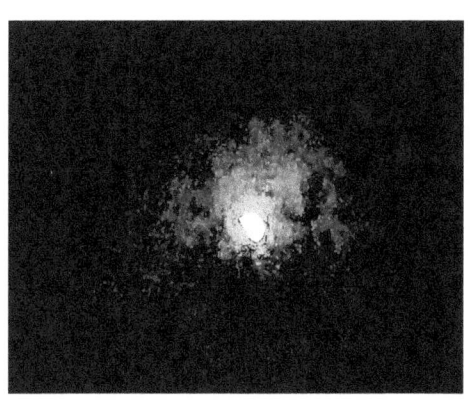

You may not hear my voice but I ask that you hear my words.

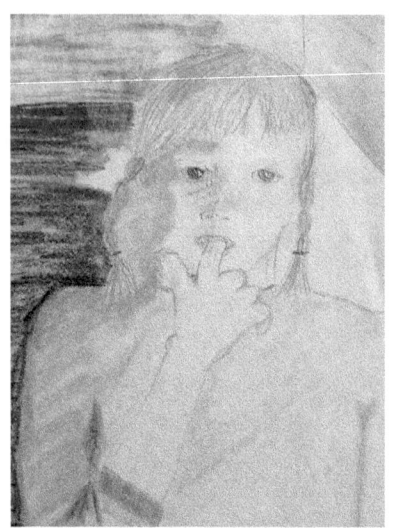

IF ONLY YOU COULD
HEAR HER SING

I was quite sure that my request to Sunshine House (a local nursing home recently making national headlines) in an attempt to shadow its employees for a "novel" I was writing would be met with anger and defensiveness. With stories of missing or injured elders and allegations of neglect by nursing home employees, I would have expected it.

Rather, there was excitement, as everyone eagerly anticipated the potential for their names to be included in a book that may be read by thousands, and therefore allowing them to be remembered forever. This reaction made me somewhat embarrassed to be a member of the human race. Was there no dignity or pride? Had it really all just come down to egotism? To be perfectly fair, my own obsession wasn't much better. However, with my own aging parents and the elderly parents of my close friends, I found it difficult not to seek out answers.

Sunshine House, whose tag line was, "a home where the sun always shines," had been in the news more than once in the last several years. Most recently for the freezing death of an elderly woman, who had triggered the alarm as she escaped to the courtyard. But shift employees had ignored the alarm, and she wasn't able to get back in. I wanted to know how this could happen. What kind of people worked in such places? Sunshine House wasn't a one-star nursing home but a small four-star facility that advertised exceptional service and staff.

My first visit was an unexpected pleasure. A cheery vestibule, live plants that sat in a rock garden with grow lights to keep them at the perfect temperature despite the cold outside air. There was no smell of urine, or the overpowering smell of bleach. A forgettable young woman at the reception desk directed me to the second floor nurse's station to meet the director, Katy Long. I took the elevator, wanting to see if it, too, was clean. Although it was almost lunchtime there was no one around. The elevator door opened to reveal a lovely corridor with bright colors and warm lighting. To the right was a small lounge with a large-screen television. Jerry Springer was on and the volume amplified for the hard of hearing. To the left was another lounge with a floor-to-ceiling birdcage filled with small, colorful, singing birds. There was a bookcase half-full of books, puzzles, and board games that stood in the corner. Both of the lounges were occupied by residents, most of them were in wheelchairs or had a decorated walker close by. Most of them were women. Other than the screaming guests on Springer, no one seemed to be talking to anyone else and there was certainly no staff around. I walked past the group on the right and could feel a few of them curiously staring at me as I made my way down the hall to the nurse's station.

Along the way, I turned my head right to left, trying to see into the rooms that lined the hall. Some had doors open more than others and I could see people sitting in chairs or lying in bed. It didn't appear that the brightness of the hall carried into the rooms.

Katy Long greeted me at the nurse's station with a yellow-toothed smile and a pudgy extended hand, whose manicured nails were painted fuchsia and whose fingers were full of gaudy cut-jeweled rings. She was a short heavyset woman who appeared to be in her early forties. She could have been much older but turned out to be even younger as I would later discover. She wore her dyed red hair in a pixie, making her face appear fatter than it was. With dangling faux emerald earrings and a bright red jacket, she was a bad impersonation of a Christmas tree. Her black elastic-banded pants were a meager attempt to appear the businesswoman. She was more than prepared and visibly excited to show me around and brag about her facility. As we walked around, she gave me the standard sales pitch. I was told about the daily activities: bingo, movies, arts and crafts; a lecture series was also included. For those residents who were more able-bodied than others, there were monthly field trips if the weather permitted. She opened doors to bright rooms that were empty as she continued to point out that Sunshine House had its own movie theater, beauty salon, and with a laugh, she added, barber shop. They had the very best of nutritionists and chefs. They always had a minimum of forty-five full-time employees to serve the ninety-eight residents, an impressive number.

We made a fast trip to the third floor where there was a small lounge with an older and smaller television set. There was only one older woman in the lounge and she seemed to be asleep in one of the chairs, her walker not within reach. The quick walk down the hall revealed most of the doors were closed and I wasn't shown any additional rooms for daily activities that she had so proudly pointed out on the second floor. When I began to question, Katy glanced at her watch, mentioning that we'd have to finish up because she had another meeting in five minutes. I pressed her to see the fourth floor but she was quick to explain that three and four were identical. With such a quick walk through the third floor and such an obvious discrepancy from two, I knew when I came back, I'd be making a visit to the fourth floor a priority. Katy's handshake goodbye felt more like a rag doll than a human hand, but her smile and invitation to make Sunshine House available for me to visit anytime and for as long as I wanted actually seemed genuine. I waited a few weeks, gathering my notes, my stories, and my nerve before I returned. On my return, I learned that the girl behind the desk, Alison, was a nineteen-year-old high school dropout who had replaced her mom, who had retired from the job she had held since Sunshine House opened in 1972. She was much more talkative than that first day. She had heard that I would be visiting often and that I was writing a book. She was so excited. She wanted to know if she could help me in anyway. She wrote poems, she told me. I thanked her and filed her offer in my memory.

That first day was a Wednesday. I got there at seven fifteen a.m., deciding to roll up my sleeves and offer to help. Those residents who could, wheeled themselves or walked with assistance to the cafeteria on the first floor. The others, maybe fifteen in total were taken by wheelchair to the atrium where tables were set up dining-room style. These were the residents who needed assistance in eating and had visitors, on a regular basis. As I would learn, every resident had a file and every file included the resident's likes and dislikes, relatives with relationship and names, sometimes even including ages. It also listed visitors who weren't relatives, like clergy, friends, and church volunteers. Details were kept of the times of visits and on what day. Every file also included financial responsibility.

All the residents on the second floor had regular visitors. All of the residents on the second floor were clean and kept busy, not necessarily active but always busy. The staff on the second floor were the cream of the crop: the registered nurses, the college students, the compassionate goal setters and achievers. The second floor was what Katy Long professed Sunshine House to be. The second floor was where I stayed for several weeks, happy to be included in staff chitchat, gossip, and after-work drinks. I was happy to be able to assist with feedings and serving, movie days, and crafts. Most of all, I enjoyed the looks on the residents' faces when they played bingo or had Devon entertain them. Devon was a thirty-five-year-old washed-up comedian. Devon spent years moving from L.A. to Vegas to New York and everywhere in between, trying to get a break. But he just wasn't funny. The rejections had taken their toll; I could see it in the premature crow's eyes and grey hair that he tried to dye with a cheap black at-home kit that made it look purple. Devon whose own down-and-out luck had brought him to Sunshine

House where he was now a star. Devon, who flirted with the women and played matchmaker with the few men who resided there. Devon, who made the residents remember, remember before, before Sunshine House.

Still, it was the gossip that finally brought me back to reality and what my role was at Sunshine House. So after several weeks, I decided it was time to get to know the staff and residents on the fourth floor. I was not too concerned about third floor, but the fourth floor intrigued me. It was the gossip that had circulated over the years that caused them to warn me that I should watch my back and that I shouldn't ever go with a full stomach, maybe a good opportunity to lose that extra five pounds I had gained hanging out with the staff and residents on two.

On my first day to the fourth floor, staff were in the process of moving Mabel from the third floor into her new room on four. Something about her tugged at me, her kind eyes, which even behind her glasses didn't hide their smile. She had beautiful skin and she was singing, her arms dancing about rhythmically. She had a cast on her left leg, which was elevated and extended, making it difficult to navigate her wheelchair. The fourth floor was like walking into the twilight zone. It was nothing like two. Garbage was left in the hall bin, and the laundry bin smelled more like shit than urine, which was left in the atrium next to the residents' dining area. This was what I had expected when I had first come to Sunshine House. Not the sterile routine and conscientious staff I had spent the last month and a half with.

Most of the doors were closed and there was no one in the halls or the small lounge area, which was more like an empty closet with a small television shoved in the corner. But the bright walls with oddly painted murals and large paper flowers lining the halls made it obvious that thought and time had been spent on the appearance.

I sat down and waited for someone, anyone. I saw Mabel's file on the counter of the unattended nurse's station. The visitor portion mentioned she had a daughter who visited every Thursday but the notes indicated she hadn't been there at all in the last four months. I had learned in my weeks on two that if residents stopped having visitors after two months, they were moved to the third floor and if it was four months or longer, they were moved to four. Looking around, I was beginning to understand.

It wasn't too long before a few young women joined each other in the hall giggling, pushing a wheelchair with a woman whose purple hair was spiked and bright red lipstick curled in the corners of her mouth to form a perpetual smile. She held her hands in her lap, showing off what appeared to be newly painted bright pink fingernails. No one said anything; instead, we sort of just stared at one another. I gathered my things and left, but as I walked to the elevator and could still hear Mabel singing, I somehow looked forward to returning fresh the next day.

When I returned to the fourth floor, I immediately heard Mabel's singing. She sat in her wheelchair behind her closed door. I attempted to introduce myself, but she was in her own world. I just listened for a while. She wasn't singing songs but instead, conversations. Conversations full of details about her past. I was intrigued and also found myself a bit obsessed. There was so much to gather and piece together. Words in song spanning decades, pieces of a tapestry quilted together, pieces of her memory, which kept her singing. Singing which I found I couldn't stop listening to.

It seemed that Mabel's singing was not as appreciated by the staff. Most of the fourth floor staff were dropouts: high school, college, vocational school, and/or society. Most of them had trouble holding a job, communicating, and fitting in. But on the fourth floor of Sunshine House, they had each found their niche.

There was Abigail, whose waist-length thick blond hair and robust figure, not to mention choice of horizontally striped scrubs, made her appear even shorter and heavier than her four feet nine frame.

Abigail changed her nail color daily, I think sometimes several times a day. She carried around a small plastic case, which was full of manicuring tools and what seemed like hundreds of different nail polish colors. Every day, she would choose a resident or two who she would spend hours shaping and painting their finger and toe nails. Sometimes she would even do theirs or both. Abigail said Gerty from Pekin liked to start the day out loud so she painted her nails with bright colors and ended the day with soft tones, at "her request." Gerty hadn't spoken a word in three years, but Abigail insisted she spoke to her all the time, telling her what color to put on each day.

And, I'm not sure where Melanie found black uniforms—perhaps she sewed them herself; she seemed creative enough. Her hair was as black as her uniform and so straight that I believed she pressed it with the same meticulousness she did her uniforms. I don't think I ever saw her wear anything but black, including her lipstick and nail polish. But when it came to the residents, it was all about color, variety, and height. Melanie was a wannabe hairstylist whose own choices prevented her from hearing anyone else's. She loved working at Sunshine House. She especially loved working on the fourth floor, where as long as her "brood" was happy, so to speak, "anything goes" and so was she. One day, I might see Evelyn with silver hair beautifully styled like Greta Garbo, or Sylvia with an orange and green bouffant. Usually, it was Agnes who Melanie liked to experiment with most. It was that mohawk she had previously styled, that she sometimes covered with wigs of various textures and lengths, wigs that Agnes liked to change as often as one would change their clothes.

Then there was Katrina. Katrina was beautiful; her green eyes a contrast to her olive skin. There was not a part of her that didn't scream perfection. I was sure she might actually be a model part-time. Katrina didn't talk, at least not to the other staff, but if one was quiet and careful not to disturb her, one would hear her cooing as she dressed and undressed residents. Like giant dolls, Katrina took great pride in picking out their outfits. Making certain everything was clean and that everything matched. She carried extra pairs of colored socks with her daily, and usually a matching scarf of some sort. She was always so careful when placing arms in sleeves, pulling up pants, and smoothing skirts, which was in great contrast to her manipulating them to a pose of her choosing, where she would leave them for hours and explode if anyone attempted to move them in the very least. However, it was Grace who was the most surprising. Grace was just plain Grace. There was nothing truly unusual about her, not someone who would stand out or who one could even describe. But it was Grace, artistic, sensual Grace, whom the residents longed for. Grace who was the one called when a diaper needed changing, or a resident had had an accident and needed cleaning. Grace who came to work each day with an apron full of colored boa feathers attached to long flexible sticks. The bright pink, blue, orange feathers falling open as if bouquets of freshly cut flowers. And by the end of each day, they were gone. No one ever knew exactly what she did with them because they were never found and no one had the nerve to ask. I think that everyone was just happy that Grace actually enjoyed her tasks, ones no one else wanted. Not even Katrina.

Additionally, there were others, Ashley, Sandra, Karl, Timothy (not Tim). They all had their quirks, but like everyone working on the fourth floor, they had a level of compassion that for some seemed to be the true sun behind Sunshine House. They were the threads that wove the fabrics together, making peace, the past with the present.

It was a compassion, however, that came with conditions and Mabel was not one who liked their rules. Everyone and everything seemed to make her agitated. Grace didn't even want to change Mabel; she did but always with complaints. Melanie, who would have loved to style her beautiful grey hair, attempted it once, only to be spit on. Katrina had tried to dress her in the new outfits that were sent in the mail by her daughter. The daughter who could never visit, at least remembered. But to Mabel, it was a memory that she could not grasp. For like her songs, the memories seldom, if ever, included the present. But a face, a familiar touch, a visitor—that would have mattered.

When she sang, "Where is she, where is she, the littlest girl I love..." I could feel her pain. For Katrina though, these clothes were a touch of heaven. They were always more fashionable than the other residents had and were already color coordinated. But with the pain Mabel seemed to be in from the broken leg and her constant flailing of her arms, it was a chore, not fun. So Katrina only dressed her if no one else was available. Abigail, in fact had wanted to fix her nails—which always appeared to have feces in them—just if even to clean them. But again, the flailing made it impossible to do so without causing pain to both Mabel and Abigail. In fact, any attempt to move her or constrain her made her scream and had resulted in two sets of broken glasses. Mabel's ongoing discomfort and uncooperativeness had even been reported to Katy, whose response I was later to learn was to just leave her alone. Katy, who had no idea I was still "observing," also suggested that I finish up so that I wouldn't disturb the staff's routine any further. I could tell she was quite irritated when she saw me on the fourth floor. It was difficult for me to oblige, but without causing too many questions, I promised to finish up by the end of the week, thanking her for the opportunity.

With difficulty and sadness, I said my goodbyes, unsure when I'd return. But Mabel's singing played in my head and a week later, I found myself returning, this time as a visitor. It was so good to hear Mabel's singing as I got off the elevator, but I wasn't prepared for what I saw. Instead of her arms flailing in dance, they were crossed in front of her chest, making her appear to be angry, defiant. When I tried to move them, I realized that they had badly contracted and could not be straightened. Had I not noticed prior? Could I have done something to keep her flexible, or was I too to blame? Even with my guilt, it was

Mabel who kept me coming back, whose singing conversations drew me in. For weeks, I came back to visit and I hated that her door was always closed, that she was always left alone. Usually, I'd find her without her glasses, just staring into space, unable to see anything or understand why she had been left there, wherever there was.

During the Christmas holiday, I stayed home, baking and preparing the house for my own mother and father, for my children's visits. I suppose it shouldn't have surprised me when after being away for several weeks, I returned to a quiet fourth floor. Getting off the elevator, I immediately heard the silence. My heart sank as I wandered down the hall to her room, praying all the way that she was just asleep. What I found was Mabel lying in her bed, appearing nothing more than a skeleton. Her dentures had been removed and her eyeglasses lay on the sink. I was told she had refused to eat. That Katy had indeed said to leave her alone. And it was too much work not to. Mabel wasn't singing anymore. I could barely make out her voice at all. I put her glasses on her like I always did and tried to give her some water through a straw. She looked at me with those same kind eyes that I remembered the first day I met her and I'm sure she smiled. I didn't stay. I learned Mabel died alone that night.

Some days I miss the time I spent at Sunshine House; they were an education. For the most part, I believe the employees cared, that it was the leadership of administrators like Katy Long who caused the most pain. They were the ones guilty of the stories that filled the news. I missed Mabel's songs, songs whose words taught me the importance of listening. I thank Mabel for that gift which I use when I listen to my own parents who often ramble or take an especially long time to finish that thirty-second story, the one I've heard ten times over. I'll miss Mabel.

I can't help but wonder if her daughter ever heard her sing.

When physical pleasures allow one to fly and
material pleasures bring laughter to the soul,
is there
still hope that the spirit can be free?

When you find that someone who makes your heart truly sing, never let them go.

BOOK CLUB DISCUSSION POINTS

1. How did you experience these stories? Did one particular story immediately draw you in or conversely take you a while to connect with?

2. Which character did you find most likeable? Why?

3. Which character made you struggle with in any way? Why?

4. Would you like to meet any of the characters – primary or secondary, and what would you say to them if given the opportunity?

5. Many of these stories feature interactions between parents and daughters? Is there a common theme that you can connect?

6. Which characters do you particularly admire or dislike? What are their primary characteristics?

7. Did any of the stories make you uncomfortable and what was it about those stories or characters that evoked that response?

8. In The Closet, what motivates Lexi's actions? Do you think those actions are justified or ethical?

9. Consider the ending of The Closet, did you expect it or were you surprised? Was it manipulative? Was it forced? Was it neatly wrapped up--too neatly? Or was the story unresolved, ending on an ambiguous note?

10. If you could rewrite the ending, would you? Why or why not.

11. Looking at Girls Night, does the book remind you of your own life? What made these characters relatable or distant from your life?

12. What would you imagine the author is trying to say about women's relationships in Girls Night?

13. In the Perfect Load there is an underlying sibling struggle. How does this compare with other sibling relationships in literature or the arts?

14. Have you ever had someone in your life that made you question yourself? How would you compare or contrast that situation to Miranda and her sister?

15. Is the end in Saying Goodbye predictable? Why or why not? What would you do if you wanted to "say goodbye."

16. Do you think that Alice's plan is any better than her friend, Kate, who committed suicide without a note? How does "If Only You Could Hear Her Sing" reflect the place of seniors in our communities? Do you agree with this portrayal?

17. Why did the author choose to "staff" the 4th floor with dropouts? What is their role in this story? Do you think the author is trying to make any type of statement and if so, what?

18. "Fading Frost" contains some graphic depictions. Are these necessary to the story? Why or Why Not?

19. How would you characterize the mother in "Fading Frost?" Is she a believable character? What brings you to that conclusion?

20. In more than one story there is a secondary theme of struggling marriages. How accurately do you feel that these relationships are portrayed? How would you respond differently than the characters reacted?

21. Several characters have collections or keepsakes that are significant to them. Which characters have such items and what is the role that they play in the story?

22. Could you relate the themes of any of these stories with current movies or television programs? How so?

23. Can you identify a theme for each story? How do the individual themes relate to the larger themes of this collection – or is there no discernable theme for the collection? Why or Why Not?

24. Fading Frost is told from different perspectives. Does that fit with the other stories in the collection and what leads you to that conclusion?

25. Do you feel that each story in the collection is of equal importance, or is one more or less impactful? What brings you to that conclusion?

26. Is there a particular story that you would want to see as an entire novel? Why? How would you see the story progressing? Would you put the stories in a different order? Which order and why?

27. This author has chosen to weave poems and artwork throughout the book. How does that add or detract to this collection?

28. Is there a quote, poem or drawing that was particularly impactful to you? What about that item was most important?

29. Would you recommend this book to other readers? To your close friend? How would you describe it?

30. If you were to talk with the author, what would you want to know?

www.ingramcontent.com/pod-product-compliance
Lightning Source LLC
Chambersburg PA
CBHW070332130626
46556CB00007B/2833